Bushwhackers

*Happy reading!
Will Davis
(Dave Bushmire)*

Will Davis

Outskirts Press, Inc.
Denver, Colorado

Bell County Bushwhackers
All Rights Reserved
Copyright © 2007 Will Davis
V2.0

Cover Image © 2007 JupiterImages Corporation
All Rights Reserved. Used With Permission.

Outskirts Press
http://www.outskirtspress.com

ISBN-13: 978-1-4327-0832-0

Outskirts Press and the "OP" logo are trademarks belonging to
Outskirts Press, Inc.

Printed in the United States of America

Dedicated to my wife Melba whose support and advice helped bring Lance Kincaid to life.

CHAPTER 1

Lance Kincaid tossed another chunk of wood on the fire to help take the chill off the evening breeze. As the fire flared and the burning embers swirled toward the night sky, he instinctively turned his gaze away from the flames to allow himself to see into the darkness that so closely reminded him of his past. It had been eighteen months since that day at Five Forks, Virginia. On the afternoon of April 1, 1865, General Sheridan called up two of General Custer's brigades to engage General Pickett's Confederate infantry on a rise just north of the village.

Lance had served as a cavalry captain with one of the Union brigades. He had led his unit at Five Forks in a final charge to dislodge the Virginians from the high ground. It was a crisp, foggy day with a light breeze, visibility coming and going as the air currents moved the mist over the battlefield. He was guided more by the sound of enemy fire than by sight. Without warning, Lance found himself surrounded by Rebel infantry as he attempted to disable the Rebs' artillery pieces. The air hung heavy with the smell of gunpowder, and the sound of the artillery was deafening. As he approached the canons, the fog and smoke cleared just enough to give him a glimpse of the Rebs. He saw the smoke from the rifle pointed at him. An instant later he felt his horse drop out from under him. Violently thrown headfirst into a large oak tree, Lance pitched forward as the horse dropped to the ground.

It was months before Lance regained consciousness. He found himself recuperating near Nashville, Illinois, at the home of a farmer, suffering six broken ribs, a fractured left leg and a bullet wound to his left shoulder. More significantly, a concussion left him with no memory of the event or anything before it. He knew little more than his name which he found out from Cord Schroeder, the farmer looking after him.

The Union officer who brought Lance to the farm told Cord that Lance had shown up at a Union field headquarters in early 1863 and volunteered for the cavalry. He was quickly recognized as a "take charge" natural leader and an accomplished horseman. His ability with the handgun and the long rifle was the envy of the entire unit, and it was obvious that guns had been a big part of his past. After a year of service he advanced to the rank of captain. Not prone to small talk, little was known about him. After the accident he was transferred to a field hospital, and then moved to the home of the Illinois farmer, who offered to look after Lance until he was back on his feet. It was six months before Lance was strong enough to begin earning his keep.

It was not unusual for families to take in soldiers that needed rehabilitation after the Civil War, and Lance was fortunate to be taken in by Cord and Johanna Schroeder, who lived just north of town. The little community was made up mostly of folks who had come to America from Germany by way of New Orleans. Many of the nearby villages were named after towns in Germany. Church services were held in German, followed by an English service. Cord and Johanna were first-generation immigrants. They had a two-hundred-acre farm and a farmhouse that could accommodate Lance and the family as they nursed him back to health.

During the early weeks of Lance's recovery Johanna and Cord would sit and talk with Lance. They shared their past with Lance and talked about their son who they lost in the war. They tried to ask questions of Lance that they thought might trigger his memory, but had no luck. Lance was very thankful to have the Schroeders to look after him and although he had little to share about himself, he enjoyed hearing about the life of Johanna and Cord.

Lance's recovery was timely, since the death of their son left Cord in need of help on the farm.

Cord's farm had 80 acres of cultivated land and 120 acres of timber. It became Lance's job to begin clearing the 120 acres. Day after day Lance kept focused on doing a good job for Cord and on his desire to recover his past. He took little time off, and his only socializing was after the evening meal with Cord and Johanna. The Schroeders had a fine collection of books and each night Lance would select one and read by candlelight for an hour before turning in. His favorite was "The Complete Works of Shakespeare."

He particularly enjoyed Johanna. She seemed to hold a place in his heart. He wondered if perhaps she reminded him of his mother. She came across as a hardheaded woman with a mindset and she tried to hide her caring side. Johanna did her share of work and then some around the farm, and there was no question where she stood on issues that concerned her.

Cord, for his part, found Lance to be a hand with the axe and the crosscut saw. He worked out an agreement with Lance to do the clearing for his keep and to share profits from the sale of the timber. As weeks turned into months, Cord found himself growing very fond of Lance. It was obvious that this young man was ingrained with a strong sense of right and wrong, an appreciation for the kindness of others, and the will to stand his ground when he knew he was in the right. He tried to control his attachment for Lance, since he was sure, one day soon, the young man would be leaving to search for his identity. He knew that Lance could not become the son he had lost.

In a few months Lance's six foot two inch broad-shouldered frame began to fill out. He now weighed 230 pounds, and his work with the axe had given him a powerful upper body. His physique, deep blue eyes, and coal-black hair drew the attention of those around him. The long hours of hard physical work and the fine cooking of Johanna brought Lance up to a hard and powerful body but, his loss of memory continued to make him feel incomplete.

He was also troubled by a recurring dream. In that dream, he would see himself in a Confederate uniform being attacked by a Union cavalry lieutenant, whose face he could clearly see just before the lieutenant struck. Lance looked around to see that all of the Confederate soldiers were spitin' images of himself. At that point Lance would wake up in a cold sweat, making no sense of this strange fantasy

After hours of swinging an axe one hot summer afternoon, Cord invited Lance to join him for a beer at the tavern in Nashville. At first Lance declined, but Cord was persistent, and said he would sure appreciate his company. Lance finally acquiesced and went back to the house to clean up for his first trip to town.

"Mind your drinking," Johanna said as they walked toward the buckboard. Cord nodded his head without looking back. They climbed aboard the wagon and headed for Wood's Tavern.

"You'll find the tavern an interesting gathering place," Cord said as they rolled along. "It was built in the 1820s by John Wood. He located it smack on the Shawnee–St Louis Trace. John does a little farming, but mostly he tends to the tavern. Word is that ol' Abe Lincoln stayed in one of the tavern's rooms some years back. Being on the trace, the tavern entertains most every kind of transient you can imagine. John will cotton to you, beings as how he was a Union major and you were a Union captain."

"I would just as leave you didn't mention my military experience, Cord."

Cord shrugged. "Sure, have it your way, Lance."

Lance felt that bringing up his military background would lead to questions that he couldn't begin to answer.

As they tied up at the tavern, Lance noticed two salty horses at the hitching post. They looked to Lance like they had been ridden hard and poorly tended to. Their hooves were split and in need of a good trimming and a set of shoes. Whoever rode them didn't have enough consideration to take some tension out of the cinches while they were not being ridden. The dried salt told Lance that they had been standing there for some time. By the looks of the gear, the riders were not locals. Lance had little respect for men who would treat their mounts the way these horses had been treated. He hadn't met these men, but he already knew he didn't like them.

Lance and Cord went up the three wooden steps, walked across the boardwalk, and pushed open the swinging doors. Without thinking, Lance stepped to the side of the door and surveyed the large room. There was a large oak bar with a mirror that ran the length of the wall. Standing at the bar, a person would have a good view of the room in the mirror. 'That's a fact worth remembering,' thought Lance. There were six round tables, each with four wooden chairs, and a potbelly stove off in one corner. Cord and John exchanged greetings. John was a lean gent in his fifties with graying hair and mutton chop side burns. He looked to be one to walk the river with. Cord ordered two beers and introduced Lance to John.

"Lance is staying with Johanna and me for a spell to give a hand with clearing some land for farming."

Cord and John exchanged some small talk until another customer needed attention. Then Lance and Cord took their beers and moved to one of the empty tables. Lance selected a chair that placed him facing the door with his back to the wall. Although Lance seemed to do it without thinking, John Wood noticed the maneuver.

Lance took in his surroundings as he lifted his glass. One table was filled with four men playing poker, another with four men eating and discussing their day on the trace. His eyes fell on two ruffians at the end of the bar who were about three drinks beyond their limit. As he eyed the two, he thought they looked like trouble waiting to happen. Lance found himself taking in their movements, size, and, what they were wearing. He paid particular attention to the navy revolvers tucked in their belts, and the knives in their boots. They were dirty, unkempt, and smelled worse than last week's fish. It was not difficult to conclude that these were the owners of the two neglected horses out front. They drank up and turned to leave.

"That will be one dollar, boys," John Wood said.

"Put it on our tab," one of the men replied.

"I deal in pay as you go," replied John.

The man closer to John drew his revolver, cocked it, pointed it at John, and said, "Then change your deal."

Lance casually got up from the table and walked calmly toward the men. He drew their attention, but not being armed, he seemed to pose no threat to them.

"Stay out of this, pretty boy," the nearer man growled.

"I just wanted to explain to Mr. Wood here that he must have misunderstood you gentlemen. He thought you were trying to run out on the tab."

"We don't run from nothin', but we ain't paying for his rotgut booze."

By this time, Lance was only two feet from the near man. As the man reached for his revolver, Lance stepped in and threw his full body behind his huge right fist. The blow landed squarely on the troublemaker's nose. His body slammed against the bar rail. His eyes rolled back in his head as he slowly slumped to the floor. That punch and the sound of bones being flattened against the man's face distracted his companion long enough for John Wood to reach across the bar and knock the gun from his hand. As it skidded across the wood floor, the man left standing reached down for the knife in his boot. On the way down, his face met with Lance's heavy left boot. The kick straightened him up. Before he reached full height, Lance landed an uppercut to his flabby midsection. The man crumbled like a building razed with dynamite.

Both men lay out cold and bleeding on the tavern floor. Lance moved to the mouthy one, took a dollar from his vest pocket, flipped it to John, and said, "Paid in full."

"Much obliged, Lance," John said.

"I just didn't like the odds," replied Lance.

"I don't believe I've ever seen anybody move faster than you did. Your pappy must have taught you well."

"I surely guess he did," replied Lance, as he tried without success to remember his father. Had his father taught him? Was his response a natural reaction, or from experience? How did he so easily size up the troublemakers? Had he been one himself? So many questions and so far no answers.

John put his hand on Lance's shoulders. "I think you best arm yourself if you're gonna hold your ground like you just did."

Lance replied calmly, "Those kind are all talk. What they are speaks so loud it's hard to hear what they say."

"Just the same, in these times a man needs to be able to defend himself. That's the Hawthorne brothers from down in the Ozarks that you just laid out. I fear you haven't heard the last of them."

"I hope you're wrong, but I guess that'll be up to them. I do figure a body should own a gun just in case the need arises. It looks as though now is the time to give it a little more thought."

John reached under the bar and brought up a Colt 44-40 revolver, holster, and a belt full of cartridges.

"I owe you, Lance. Take this and pay me when you come by the money. It belonged to one of the officers who served with me. He decided he had no use for it when he turned preacher and started a Lutheran church over in New Minden."

From the second Lance touched the handgun, he knew he was no stranger to its use. The outfit felt good as he strapped it on his hip. Cinching up the belt, he realized it was a natural part of him, a part he had been missing until now. He flipped the thong off the hammer, drew the revolver, and checked the loads. It was loaded except for the cartridge that would rest under the hammer. The butt was a good fit for his large hand, and he liked the balance.

"A weapon is only as good or as bad as the person using it," John said. "Use it in good conscience, Lance."

"That I will," replied Lance. He nodded toward the Hawthorne brothers. "Do you need some help getting rid of these customers?"

"No thanks. I'll just have the sheriff let them sleep it off in the jail. He can decide if he wants to call the 'sawbones' and have this one's nose fixed," John replied.

Cord and Lance finished their beer and headed back to the farm.

"You took a chance back there," Cord said.

"Not really," replied Lance. "The booze had affected their reaction time as well as their good judgment. That's why I limit myself to a beer now and then. I imagine many a man has been done in by taking on too much liquor. If a body is gonna survive these days, he best be playing with a full deck."

Both men fell silent for the remainder of the ride home. Lance was preoccupied thinking about John's tavern. Since it was located on the trace, there would be a lot of travelers stopping over, travelers who might drop some clues as to his past. Lance decided he would spend some of his free time there, taking in the small talk of the customers.

******

In the months that followed, Lance visited John's tavern as often as he could, studying people and listening to their trials and tribulations. They came from all walks of life, with a full range of experiences. He envied those who could speak so easily of their past.

One evening while Lance was nursing his beer at the tavern, his eyes met those of a man coming through the swinging doors.

"Lance! Lance Kincaid!" the man said as he walked up to Lance's table.

Although he had no idea who the man was, Lance recognized him immediately as the Union officer from his dream. The man appeared to be younger than Lance, slight of build and about five eight. He was wearing his leftover union breeches and a wool shirt that had seen better days. His clean shaven face and cropped hair made him look younger than his years. Lance sat in a state of shock and tried to gather his wits enough to reply to the gentleman's greeting. For lack of a better response, Lance said, "Have we met before?"

Surprised, the stranger replied, "You're putting the shuck on me, partner. Are you telling me you don't remember me, after all the time we spent together in Virginia, cleaning those Rebels's plow?"

Lance collected himself, invited the man to join him, and proceeded to explain how he had lost all recall when he was wounded. Lance could hardly control his emotions, realizing that he had finally made a connection with his past. The man introduced himself as Chad Forrest, an ex-Union cavalry officer who fought at Five Forks alongside Lance.

"The last time I saw you it was in the fog on the morning we hit the Reb artillery unit on that ridge north of Five Forks. We took'em out, but it cost us dearly as you well remember, or I guess you don't."

Lance wrinkled his brow as in deep thought and said, "When you called to me at the door I recognized you as the Union officer in my dreams, but nothing comes back to me about the charge."

"You're having dreams about me?" Chad asked.

"It's more like a nightmare. I keep seeing you as a Union officer and all of the Rebel soldiers around me look just like me. Then I wake up in a cold sweat trying to make sense of it."

"Well, I was close by when you went down, but I was horsebelly deep in Rebs and they darn sure didn't look like you," Chad replied.

Try as he might, Lance still could not remember any of the particulars that Chad described, and he had so many questions, he didn't know where to start. It was not long into the conversation before Lance realized that this chance meeting was going to be of little help in recovering his past. After a few unanswered questions from Lance, Chad said, "You know, Lance, you were always a loner and not one for idle chatter. Your focus was always on the task at hand and how best to handle it. If it wasn't for picking up your mail occasionally, I wouldn't have known anything about you."

"What do you mean?" replied Lance.

"Well, you received several letters from your pa. At least you said it was your pa. I noticed the name and return address. They were from a Mr.

Kincaid, and postmarked Belton, Texas. You said he had a ranch near Belton."

Encouraged by this bit of information, Lance peppered him with questions about other possible kin, his mother, and the ranch, but Chad knew no more than what he had just shared. Chad spent the next hour reliving his war experiences and describing the fighting that he and Lance did together serving under Custer. It seemed to Lance it would have taken ten wars to cover all the tales Chad recounted. Nothing he said, however, brought forth any images or details to Lance's mind.

Finally, as the evening wore on, Lance thanked Chad for the information and explained that he had to be on his way. The ranch in Belton wasn't much to go on, but at least it was a start. Lance had to get to his father's ranch in Texas. There were a lot of details to work out before he could leave, on his long ride to Texas and suddenly he was impatient to start.

"I owe you Chad," he said, shaking his hand. "If you ever need a favor, look me up in Texas at the Kincaid Ranch."

"Actually, Lance, you could do me a favor right now."

"Name it."

"You could let me ride with you to Texas."

Lance wasn't prepared for such a request. His mind raced through the advantages and drawbacks of having a partner for his trip. His first thought was, 'I work alone and I prefer to travel alone'. Before he could answer, Chad explained, "You see, I'm kinda on the run. Not from the law, from the Regulators."

"What are the Regulators?"

"I thought I knew what they were until several weeks ago," replied Chad. "The Union government organized them, either officially or unofficially, just after the war. Their stated purpose was to see that the Confederate property owners were fairly treated during the Reconstruction of the South. It seemed like a good cause, and they offered thirty dollars per month, plus keep. Come to find out, a few of them had irons of their own in the fire. It became clear to me they were hidin' behind the government and using their resources to cheat property owners out of their land and businesses. They were demanding sky-high taxes of the Confederates. When they couldn't pay, they took possession of their property. When I discovered what they were up to I challenged one of the bosses of the unit. We had a bit of a disagreement, and I stomped a mudhole in him. I'm not sure he survived. I didn't wait to find out. It was a fair fight; he was twice my size.

"My daddy always said, 'Son, you're not too hefty, so you have to be quick and surprise 'em'. I guess I looked pretty hefty when I surprised that dude. The short of it is I'm not very welcome in these parts. I lost my ma and pa when I was just a youngster. I have no truck with females, so I have no ties or any other reasons to hang around."

Lance sat there quietly and rubbed his chin with his left hand, as he was prone to do when he was about to make a decision. He knew it was going to be a trip with its share of risks. It would be advantageous to have someone cover his back in case of problems with Indians, thieves, or those with adverse leanings to his own. On the other hand, he figured he would arrive in Texas without any ears, since Chad would have talked them off by then. After weighing the ups and downs of it, Lance decided to accept Chad's offer.

"Okay, 'Hefty'!" replied Lance. "On one condition. Either one of us can decide to end this partnership if it seems to be goin' sour."

"It's a deal, Lance. I guess I asked for that handle. You can call me Hefty or anything that suits you."

"Where are you calling home?" Lance asked.

"Actually, my saddle, for the time being. I'm packing all my belongin's in my saddlebags until I can find a place to light."

"I'm staying with the Schroeders on their farm just north of town. Why don't you return to the farm with me? If they can put you up, we can stay there until we get the necessary arrangements made for our trip."

"That's darn sure the best offer I've had today."

The two mounted up and headed for the farm. Although it was late fall the day was hot and humid. Before long the horses were working up a good sweat.

"We best let up on this pace. These ponies are

foaming up like a new-drawn beer," Lance said.

Chad grinned. "You may have lost your memory, but you sure haven't lost your priority to look after your mount. You were always that way in the unit. You spent more time looking after your horse than you did taking care of yourself."

"We depend on our mounts, and they're at our mercy. It seems to me we ought to show them all the care we can. Surely a day will come when our lives will depend on them." He paused, and then asked, "What happened to the horse I was riding when I was hit?"

"He was hit a lot harder then you were. He had to be put down on the spot."

"I guess that's one thing I'd just as soon not remember."

As they rode on, Lance told Hefty how the Schroeders had taken him in and nursed him back to health. He had developed a strong feeling for the couple, and would regret leaving them. He had no doubt, though, they would understand when he broke the news to them.

CHAPTER 2

When they arrived at the farm, Lance introduced Hefty to the Schroeders and explained his connection to him. Cord wasn't surprised that Lance intended to follow this slim lead to his past. As Lance had expected, they invited Hefty to stay with them until they headed out for Texas. For the next three months, Hefty helped Lance clear the land and sell lumber. By early spring they had enough of a stake between them to head for Texas.

Lance felt that having a good horse under him could make the difference between life and death. He did a lot of looking and a lot of bargaining before he settled on a fifteen-and-a-half-hands-tall bay mare whose owner declared she was a four-year-old. After a quick check of her teeth and the cavities over her eyes, he put her closer to an eight-year-old. Her age was not a concern since she was sound, in good health, and well breed. By the way she handled, Lance figured she had seen her share of those quarter-mile races that gave the quarter horse breed their name. He wasn't sure what name she went by before, but from now on she would go by Bess.

After paying for Bess, Lance had enough money left from his earnings to pay John for his revolver and pick up a 44-40 Winchester repeating rifle. Now he had a short gun and a rifle that used the same cartridges. That could be very important if he ran into some big-time trouble.

Hefty already had his weapons and his horse from the war, but he did swap his horse for one that he thought would have bottom, if an occasion should call for it. The horse was a cold blood and not much to look at. She went by the name of Pigeon Toed Toni. That about said it all. She surely was trail-smart and had hooves so hard she required no shoes. She was a mousy-dun mare about fourteen hands, and a good match for Hefty's height.

They put together the grub they thought they would need, but no more than they could pack on the horses. A lot of their eats would have to come off the land. They considered leaving out of Sedalia and down the old Shawnee Trail, but that would take them through Comanche and Kiowa country. There were other problems with that route, including the lack of U.S. Army protection.

Lance had heard a lot about a trail known as the "Chisholm Trail." It seems the trail was first blazed in the early 1860s by a rancher named Jesse Chisholm, and it was used in 1866 by Texas cattlemen to drive their cattle north to the railhead in Baxter Springs, Kansas. Unfortunately for the Texans, Baxter Springs was made up of a lot of die-hard ex-Union soldiers who hated the Texans. These Yankees often blocked the trails to the railhead and held off the Texans and their cattle until winter killed off the grass and caused the loss of most of the herds.

The following year, an ambitious young man named Joseph McCoy of Springfield, Illinois, put up some stockyards near the end of the Kansas Pacific Railroad at Abilene, Kansas. Over the next decade, McCoy faced financial challenges caused by fear of splenic fever, which longhorns were bringing out of Texas, and the resentment the Yankee farmers felt toward Texans. The longhorns were immune to the fever they carried, but it proved deadly to the northern stock. Efforts were made by the northern ranchers to prevent the Texas herds from moving north. They succeeded for some time in having a quarantine line established, across which longhorns were not permitted. In an effort to keep his cattle business flourishing, McCoy offered to pay the locals for any cattle they lost due to the fever. That offer, along with the positive economic impact the Texas drovers brought to the area, resulted in the resumption of cattle trading out of Texas.

Lance and Hefty decided to try their hand at getting to Abilene, and from there, down the Chisholm Trail to Texas. They were both good hands, and hoped to hire on with a wagon train to get from St. Louis to Abilene. There they would join up with some Texas wranglers returning home after their cattle drive.

The evening before they were to leave for Texas, Lance and Hefty saddled up and headed for Nashville for a last drink at the tavern, and to say their goodbyes to John Wood. As the two entered the tavern and walked up to the bar, Lance noticed a strained look on John's face. Looking in the mirror behind John, he immediately saw the reason. In the far-right darkened corner of the room, he saw the reflection of one of the Hawthorne brothers sitting at a table. The other brother was sitting directly behind Lance, next to the swinging door. The one at the door spoke first.

"Well, if it ain't Mr. Fancypants and his little buddy."

Lance kept both hands on the bar and replied without turning around. "I have no quarrel with you. I suggest you leave well enough alone and don't push your luck."

"I'm not countin' on luck this time, and I'm not boozed up, but I will be after I take care of some unfinished business."

Lance was too occupied to be frightened. He felt his senses come alive. He decided he would go for the first man who made a move and hope he would have time to handle the other one. Hefty glanced at Lance in the mirror and saw him slowly rub his chin with his left hand.

"I want no part of this," Hefty said, and turned for the door. At that moment, the man in the darkened corner went for his gun. Lance saw him in the mirror, turned, drew, and fired in one smooth motion. Before the man cleared his handgun from his belt, Lance's 44 bucked in his hand. A hole appeared in Hawthorne's chest just left of his breastbone. The slug drove the man over the back of his chair.

As Lance turned to face Hawthorne's brother, he found the man already on the floor as a result of a body block thrown by Hefty. The man rolled onto his left side, drew his revolver, and fired, shattering the mirror over Lance's shoulder. Before he could get off a second shot, Lance put a slug just below his hairline.

The two Hawthorne brothers were dead.

Lance felt anger well up in him. He was not concerned for the brothers. They were no-accounts. But he hated the fact that he was forced to take lives for no good reason. He also realized he had taken the action he did without thinking. It all seemed so automatic, he had not even been aware of what he was doing. He knew he must have faced similar situations before, but where, when, and what was his part in it?

Trying to stifle the questions preying on his mind, Lance turned to Hefty. "You saved my life," he said. "But I thought for a minute there you were throwing in your hand."

"I was only hoping they would think that too," replied Hefty. "I knew you were fixin' on doin' something pretty quick, and thought if I could distract one, it would give you the edge you needed. I'm no gunhand. I knew drawing on one of 'em would only buy me a bullet."

John came from around the bar and checked the two brothers. "They never knew what hit 'em," he said. "That's the second time I've seen you in action, Lance, and I have never seen anybody move like you do."

"Then you must've missed the move Hefty put on the one at the door," replied Lance.

The ruckus had attracted a crowd. John sent one of the onlookers for the sheriff. When the sheriff arrived, John recounted the incident and made it clear that it was self-defense. The sheriff was well acquainted with the brothers, and knew them to be troublemakers. He placed no charges against Lance or Hefty, and told them they were free to go. Lance offered to pay for the mirror, but John declined, saying it would have probably cost him more in the long run if the Hawthorne brothers had continued to visit his tavern. Lance bid John goodbye and thanked him for his kindness. He and Hefty mounted up and headed back to the farm.

They were about halfway to the farm when Hefty spoke. "That little dance back at the bar reminds me of the time my pappy and I were hired to do some carpentry work for the local school. I was only nine at the time, not much more than a tool-fetcher for Pa. We'd worked on the schoolhouse for a couple of days when we hit a snag. It seems there was a full-time carpenter in town who thought he should have gotten the job. Well sir, when Pa and I showed up on the job, this brute of a man stepped in front of Pa and said, 'Your work is finished, Forrest; get your tools and light out.' The guy was about twice Pa's size. Pa wasn't too hefty either. The dude scared me. Pa didn't say a word; he just turned and walked to the wagon. I figured that was the end of it. But when we got to the wagon, Pa picked up a nine-pound hammer and headed back to the ape and calmly said, 'I aim to finish the job I started. I can either walk around you or over you, your choice!' I figured the guy was going to drop us both. I guess I didn't see the look in my pa's eyes that he saw. Anyway, the guy never said a word; he just stepped aside and went about whatever other business he had to attend to."

"I'm not sure why today's run-in reminded you of that story."

"Well, I guess it's my long-winded way of saying I saw that same look in your eyes just before you made your move."

"Remind me not to play poker with you," Lance laughed. He wondered how many more stories were in his future. He figured he'd know he'd heard them all about the time Hefty started to repeat the same ones over again.

As they rode along Lance said, "Are you going

to be ready to lite out at "can see" tomorrow?

"You bet. I have all the cartridges I can carry, my bedroll is fit to be tied to my saddle, my change of shirt and socks are in my saddle bags and I believe my "can do" has caught up with my "want to".

"It sounds like you've thought about it all. How about our grub?"

"Mrs. Schroeder told me not to fret none about food. She said she would see to that."

"Are there any other arrangements you've made for the trip that you haven't shared with me?"

Hefty smiled and said, "No that's just about it."

CHAPTER 3

It was difficult saying goodbye to the Schroeders. They were the only family Lance knew, and he had become very fond of them. Still, he had to go about finding his blood kin.

Cord helped them get the saddlebags packed and their gear tied down. Johanna was nowhere to be seen until just before they were ready to mount up. She came out of the house with a large tow sack full of salt, flour, biscuits, bacon, hard-boiled eggs and a sack of hard candy she had purchased at the mercantile. She was only partially successful in holding back her tears.

"We will miss you, Lance. You certainly have become a part of our family during your stay with us. Our prayers will be with you both. I'm pleased you won't be traveling alone. Godspeed, boys. You will always have a home here if you should ever feel the need."

"Thank you, ma'am. Your kindness has meant a lot to me. As you know, you are the closest thing to family I can remember. We appreciate your prayers. I'm sure we'll need all the help we can get," Lance said, as he leaned down and kissed Johanna on the forehead.

As Hefty swung into the saddle, he looked back at Johanna and said, "I'm not much of a church-going man, but I'm sure your prayers will do us a lot more good than this rabbit's foot I carry around. I thank you for your hospitality, and I wish well for you and your husband."

Cord made no comment. He was afraid that any words would bring on tears. He shook hands with both men and waved goodbye as they rode off. With that farewell, they headed out for St Louis.

******

The first few days were uneventful. The fifty-mile trip to St. Louis took just two days. It was a good stretch to get a feel for their mounts and learn about any of their boogers. Both horses proved to be seasoned trail horses with good stamina. Bess showed her common sense when she encountered a five-foot rattlesnake on the trail. She froze at the buzz of the rattle and pricked her ears in the direction of the coiled snake. Lance drew and fired from the saddle before the rattler could muster a strike.

The head of the snake disappeared and the body went reeling down the hill and came to a stop about six feet off the trail. Both horses had been fired from before, and neither reacted to the gunshot from the saddle.

Hefty whistled. "I've seen fast before, but that's the first time I've seen anyone faster than a rattle-snake's strike," he said.

"I was just lucky I came across a slow snake."

"Was it luck you blew his head off?"

Lance just rubbed his mare's neck and moved out along the trail without saying a word.

When they reached St. Louis, there was no lack of opportunity to hire on with a wagon train. The city was humming with activity. It was the jump-off to the West. The hotels and saloons were filled with locals, prospectors, pioneers, and hunters. It had its share of prostitutes and shysters, too, trying to swindle the un-suspecting. Lance and Hefty stayed clear of any of the "quick buck" artists and concentrated on finding their ticket to Abilene. They connected up with a train headed for the Colorado Territory. The wagon master offered free meals and a wagon to sleep under in ex-change for hunting down food and helping with the setup and takedown of the wagons, morning and night. They would learn a lot about wagons, oxen, and people on the trip.

The second night on the trail with the wagon train, as everyone gathered around the fire, an over-grown farmer from Ohio named Jacob Haskell asked Lance where he was from. Lance answered back, "Bell County, Texas."

Jacob replied, "My brother was killed by a Texan. As far as I'm concerned the only good Texan is a dead Texan."Lance sized Jacob up to be about thirty years old, six foot one or two, and 275 pounds, with hands as big as sledgehammers. He had a full, dark beard that gave him an evil look, but Lance judged him to be a hardworking farmer and not much more. He carried no weapon and wore heavy farm shoes.

Lance looked back at the fire. "I guess you're entitled to your opinion," he said quietly.

"It's not just my opinion, it's the opinion of every Yankee in this train."

"Well, y'all are entitled to your opinion," Lance answered.

Hefty said, "Lance was an officer in the Union Army."

Jacob looked over at Lance and spat, "Probably changed his colors when he knew he was going to get his ass whooped."

Hefty watched Lance rub his chin with his left hand, and said under his breath, "Time to pay the fiddler."

"My motives are none of your business, sod buster," Lance said.

"Well, I'm making it my business," Jacob said as he swung a roundhouse clean from the south forty at Lance's jaw.

That full windup gave Lance more than enough

time to step inside the punch. He turned his back to Jacob, grabbed his swinging arm, stuck his leg out, and gave the farmer a hip roll that put him flat on his back. Before Jacob could collect his wits, two of his friends moved toward Lance.

"Let's keep this a fair fight, shall we, boys?" Hefty said, drawing his belt gun and holding it on the two farmers.

By now Jacob was on his feet and coming at Lance. With his head down he wrapped his arms around Lance's waist. Lance locked his fingers together and came down on Jacob's back just below his rib cage. Jacob let out a loud gasp and again fell to the ground. Once more he got to his feet, just in time to receive a crashing right hook to his jaw. The large man reeled back on his heels and over onto his back. This time he did not get up. Lance went over to the side of one of the wagons, returned with a bucket of water, and threw it in Jacob's face. Jacob shook himself back to the living and slowly got to his feet. He stood there straddle-legged, trying to keep his balance, and he showed no urge to move on Lance.

"I have my opinions and you have yours. Let's leave it at that and we'll have no more trouble," Lance said as he returned to his log by the fire. The bruised and beaten farmer returned to his wagon without a comment.

The wagon master approached Lance and asked if he could have a word with him at his wagon. Lance followed the wagon master, wondering what was in store for him.

"I just want you to know that Jacob's views are not those of most of the folks on this train," the wagon master said. "The war is over, and we would like to get on with our lives and look to the future. A lot of people, on both sides of this war, lost loved ones, and the losses and hurts aren't over by a long shot. We all have to get that behind us and move on. More foolish violence is not going to undo the wrong. You're obviously no stranger to violence, and my guess is you have had some fight training. I only ask that you try to avoid any further trouble."

"I'll do my best. I guess I have a lot to learn about people's feelings." Lance went on to explain to the wagon master about his past, as much as he knew about it, and told him why he was headed for Texas.

"You're in a tough situation, a Texan who believes in the Union cause, traveling with a Yankee on your way to Texas. That's a tough row to hoe. Let me warn you: there are a lot of bitter folks as a result of this war, and the Texans aren't the least of them. I suggest that you proceed carefully and don't draw attention to yourself until you determine which way the wind blows. The folks in Texas have been fighting Mexicans, Indians, and Yankees over the years, and they don't much trust anybody except dyed-in-the-wool Texans."

"I appreciate your concern, and I'll do my best not to cause you or your train any more trouble."

"I wish you well, friend," the wagon master replied, and the two men returned to the fire.

Lance and Hefty stayed to themselves as much as possible for the remainder of the trip to Kansas City, helping out when they were needed. They spent a lot of their time hunting, supplying the train with fresh meat. They learned how to build wagon wheels and how to fire the steel rims to create a tight fit. Some days they spent hours helping the oxen by pushing the loaded wagons through muddy ruts in the makeshift roads. They certainly felt no guilt about receiving their free meals.

While hunting game for the train, Lance decided that Hefty may not be quick with his belt gun, but he sure was a crack shot at all distances with a rifle. It was already evident that Lance had made the right decision when he agreed to allow Hefty to join him. They were hardly on their way and Hefty had already come to his rescue twice.

A month had passed since they had left Nashville. The time had passed quickly, mostly because when they weren't sleeping, they were busy helping the families on the wagon train. Their hard work and obvious concern for the wagon train families gained them the respect of most of the train members. Mostly farm folks, they were looking to come by some of that great grassland they had heard about. They carried all their worldly goods with them and all their dreams for a better life. For Lance, it was just hope to find the life he once had.

CHAPTER 4

A flare-up and a sharp series of pops from the fire brought Lance out of his deep thought and caused Hefty to jump from his bedroll.

"What was that?" Hefty murmured, half awake.

"Just the pitch in the firewood. Go back to sleep," replied Lance.

"What time is it, Lance?"

"It's near dawn," he said.

"Did you get any sleep, Lance?"

"No, been turned inside out trying to review my past six months to uncover anything that could trigger my memory. It just seems to me there is a clue somewhere in there that could put me on the right path to my past. That dream I keep having just doesn't make any sense. It must mean something."

"I hear sometimes the harder a body tries to remember something the more difficult it is to recover it. Maybe if you just try to get it out of your head it will come to you," Hefty said.

"I guess I'll never know if that works or not, because I can't begin to get it out of my head. I could be a rancher, a renegade, a rounder or any one of a number of undesirables."

"Well since you're throwing in all those R's, you might include royalty, rich, a reverend, a ranger or just a regular everyday kind of a cowpoke."

"I have to say I like your choices better than mine. What ever I am, it sure would be nice to know."

"I guess in a way I'd like to know just what I am, Hefty said. "I hadn't given it much thought until I met up with you and your predicament. I've never spent much time looking back or planning ahead. I just live out each day and let the future take care of itself. It's past time for me to take stock of myself and decide where I want to be in, say—ten years. It doesn't appear to be much worthwhile, since it takes money to get anywhere and money is one thing I've never seemed to come by."

"You just need a good woman to give you some incentive. You got all the makin's to be whatever you decide to be."

"I've no truck with females and for now I suggest we aim to get you back on track and I'll worry about me later," Hefty said

"Fair enough. We can probably do ourselves the most good by whipping up some breakfast and some coffee strong enough to float a horseshoe."

"Now you're talkin' on something that I can handle, Hefty said.

The sun was high in the east by the time they finished their breakfast of side meat, hard boiled eggs and biscuits. They broke camp, brushed down there horses, saddled up and headed south for Texas.

******

Lance and Hefty traveled with the wagon train as far as Kansas City. It was there that they heard about trouble along the Chisholm Trail. A few months earlier General Custer had led a massacre of a Cheyenne village, in which Chief Black Kettle and his wife were killed. As a result of that attack, the Kiowas and the Comanche had decided that the white man's words were not to be trusted. They began raiding white settlers on the Chisholm Trail along the Canadian and Washita rivers. Lance couldn't blame the tribes. From what he had seen and heard, the whites had certainly earned the distrust of the Indians. One treaty after another had been ignored or broken, and the violators had received little or no reprimand from the government. Still, Lance did not want to be a part of their payback. He had heard from a scout by the name of Christopher Carson that the trip would be a lot safer if they joined up with wranglers headed back to Texas.

Hefty said, "I don't have the crop of hair you have, Lance, but if it's all the same to you, I'd just as leave keep what I have. I'm all for taking the trail that will stack the odds in our favor, even though it's a crapshoot either way."

Hefty had heard that fifteen cowhands with a wagon had headed south for Texas on the Chisholm Trail just about a week before. With any luck, they could overtake them in three or four days, traveling light like they were.

The pair headed south on the trail at first light. It had been a rainy season that year and the rolling hills were covered with tall prairie grass. A norther had just blown through the week before, dropping a goodly amount of rain. That would help them track the cow-hands and judge how fresh the tracks were. As it turned out, there was no need getting directions, as the trail was well worn and easy to follow. When they came upon the sign they thought to be the cowhands, they noticed there were ruts from two wagons. Neither wagon showed the sign of much weight. One was surely the chuck wagon. The other wagon was even lighter and couldn't be carrying much cargo. It made for an easy bunch to keep track of.

After three days on the trail, they came upon an unwelcome sight. Hefty was hunting off west of the trail when he cut sign of five or six unshod ponies. After backtracking the prints, he decided that these ponies had been following them for at least the last several miles. He hightailed it back to Lance and told him what he had come across. They decided to make camp for the night in a place that would offer a measure of protection. Since the Kiowas and the Comanches were active farther south, it was a good guess these were Cheyenne. If that were true, they weren't likely to be too friendly to whites after what had happened to Black Kettle.

Lance and Hefty had plenty of ammunition and enough food for themselves, but they also had to think of food for their horses and water for man and horse. As midday approached, they spotted a bluff off to the east. At the base of the bluff was a stand of cottonwoods. As they neared, the horses picked up their pace, a good sign that there was grass or water. As it turned out, there were both. A small spring fed a shallow meadow that had a good stand of grass. The approach to the meadow was flat and wide open, with little opportunity for someone to hide. Behind the spring was a vertical bluff several hundred feet high. It wasn't likely they would find a better place to hold up.

"This is our lucky day," Hefty said.

"It won't be if we head for that spring," Lance replied. "Those six have been tailing us for the better part of the day. I was hoping they were just curious. But they made a statement when they let you cut their tracks. My guess is they're already at the spring waiting for us."

"Why didn't you tell me you spotted them, Lance?"

"Because I didn't want them to know we were onto them, and I wasn't sure you could play it out."

"What now?" Hefty asked, as he squinted into the setting sun, looking for any sign of the would-be ambush.

Lance rubbed his chin with his left hand as he shifted his weight in the saddle to check his cinch.

"We need to keep moving south along the trail at an easy pace until we pass through that saddle up ahead. Once we're out of sight, we'll kick in the spurs and get some distance between us and them. Then we'll find a spot to do a little ambushing of our own. They know this territory better than we do, so it's not going to be easy to surprise 'em."

They reached the cut in the road without any sign of movement behind them. Lance gave the signal, and they both kicked their horses into a pace that put their hat brims tight against the crown. About two miles down the trail they came to an outcropping of rocks that would afford enough cover for one man. To the west there was a swell about sixty feet high. Lance told Hefty to hold up behind the rocks and cover their back trail. Lance rolled back Bess and headed for the swell. He would be west of the trail. Lance had taught his mare to lie down on cue. He gave her that cue, and then positioned himself so he could see her ears. The sun would be to his back as he looked down on the trail. For the next thirty minutes there was no noise or movement except for the cottontail that was feeding on the sparse prairie grass along the trail. As Lance watched the cottontail he saw him lower his ears against his back and hunker down. Here they come, he thought.

Just then, he saw a moving shadow cast by the setting sun. It was them, sure enough, but they were on foot. They must have figured that Lance and Hefty had taken a stand. He counted four of them, and they were cautiously moving toward Hefty. That left two unaccounted for.

KBOOM!

It was the discharge of Hefty's fifty-caliber Hawkins. Lance saw an Indian fall forward from the rocks just east of Hefty. That's five, Lance thought. He rubbed his chin. Four down the trail, one to the east—that could mean the sixth one had circled to the west. At that instant, Lance saw his mare raise her head and prick her ears. He turned to see the sixth Indian, bow drawn and ready to release. As Lance rolled to the right, the arrow pierced his shirtsleeve and pinned his left arm to the ground. His revolver bucked in his right hand, and he saw the Indian fall to his knees and then onto his face. He had a hole in him just above the sternum, and the 44 slug came out his back, leaving a hole as big as a double eagle.

As he pulled the arrow out of the ground and back through his shirtsleeve, he heard the thunder of that Hawkins. Hefty had hit another Indian, who had reacted to the discharge of Lance's revolver, exposing himself to Hefty. From Lance's vantage point, he could see the Indian dragging himself away with a thigh wound.

Now there was a deafening silence. Lance could see no movement, no shadows. He waited another ten minutes, then gathered up his horse and scrambled down the hill to Hefty.

"Are you okay, Hefty?" Lance asked.

"I'm a darn sight better off than they are," Hefty answered back.

"You took that last one in the thigh."

"By the looks of that bloody left arm, I got by a little better than you did, pard. What happened?"

"It's just a nick. It could have been a lot worse if it hadn't been for Bess. She warned me about the Cheyenne that circled to the west just in time to allow me to dodge an arrow."

Lance removed his shirt and splashed the wound with water from his canteen. He tore the tail off a clean shirt he had in his saddlebag and tied it snug around his upper arm over the wound.

"That should do it." Lance said.

"What now?" Hefty asked.

"I think we bought us some time. They'll be tending to that wounded one and looking after their dead before they get around to us again. By that time we should be out of their reach. Let's mount up and get some distance between us and them. It will mean traveling at night, but we have an outlaw moon, so we should be able to make our way without any trouble. We better hope we come onto some water."

They turned their ponies south and headed out at a brisk trot.

"What's an outlaw moon?" Hefty asked.

"It's enough moon to see by, but not enough to make you easily seen," replied Lance.

"Where did you come by that, Lance?"

"I don't rightly know. I've been coming up with a lot of things and feelings that I have no idea where they're coming from. Maybe I'll know when we get to my pa's ranch in Bell County."

"Well, I can tell you one thing. It didn't come from Pittsburgh," Hefty replied.

"What does Pittsburgh have to do with anything?"

"That's where I'm from, and we never heard of an outlaw moon in the Pennsylvania coal mines."

"Hefty, you were a coal miner?"

"A lot of my family was, but not me. Pappy was an outside pit boss, and he wouldn't let me work down in the mine. Said it was too dangerous."

"I thought you told me your father was a carpenter."

"My pappy had more jobs than you could count. It seemed like he was always working. For a while he did carpentry on weekends and evenings, and held down that pit boss job during the weekdays. He didn't seem content unless he was working at something. As I was saying, I helped him in the shop, above ground. Mostly he had me help him with the mules. That is, once I got the hang of it."

"Once you got the hang of what?" Lance asked.

"Well, sir, I just started helping Pappy when he

asked me to hold a twitch on an old cussed mule he was trying to shoe. He put the twitch on the mule's nose, and showed me how to keep it twisted, and then he started to put shoes on the back feet of that mule. Well, I got so interested in what he was doin' I let up the tension on that twitch. Next thing I knew, Pappy was picking himself up about six feet behind the mule. 'Dang you, Chad,' he said. 'That mule has been waiting fifteen years for a chance to kick my butt and you just gave him the opportunity.' Right quick, he taught me to do the shoeing and he held the twitch."

"I'm sorry I asked", Lance replied, grinning to himself at Hefty's latest tale.

They kept an easy pace to save the horses and reduce the need for water. About an hour before sunrise, they came to a small stream and decided to hold up and give themselves and the horses a breather. They unsaddled the horses, rubbed them down with some dry grass, and hobbled them near the stand of grass that bordered the stream.

Hefty put together enough of a fire to brew some of that strong coffee he liked so well. He built the fire under an old oak so the smoke would be filtered through the leaves and would be harder to see from a distance. He quickly covered the fire when the coffee was ready. Since they had put considerable distance between themselves and the Cheyenne, they decided to catch some sleep. The excitement of the day left Lance a little on edge. Since he wasn't sleepy, he decided to take first watch. Hefty was asleep before his head hit the saddle he was using for a pillow.

Lance moved away from the camp, where he could watch their back trail and listen for sounds that were not of their own making. With any luck, they would meet up with the cowboys before the next sunset.

An hour after sunrise Hefty woke up and sat down next to Lance. "Any activity?" he asked.

"None to speak of—a few coyotes and a hoot owl."

"I've had enough sleep, Lance. You should try to get some."

"I don't feel the need for sleep just now. Let's saddle up and move on," Lance replied. He figured the farther south they were the less chance there was that the Cheyenne would follow them. Of course that also meant that there was a greater risk of meeting up with the Comanches. The Comanches were formidable enough that even the Cheyennes and the Apaches stayed shy of them.

They drank down the last of the coffee, took on some beef jerky, and headed south.

"I've been thinking, Hefty," Lance said, coming up alongside him. "That wagon master back there made a good point about our reception in Texas. We're not likely to be welcome. I think it best that we keep our personal business to ourselves, and we'll be better off not using my last name for a spell."

"Sounds like good thinking to me," replied Hefty.

That night, the two pulled into Baxter Springs,

Kansas. The small town was benefiting from a couple of nearby cattle trails and as a result, was made up of a collection of teamsters, cowboys, railroad workers, liquor dealers, gamblers, and prostitutes. As was to be expected, there were more saloons and dance halls than anything else. The dirt streets were full of activity. Wooden planks spanned the muddy areas to allow the ladies to cross without soiling their shoes. The sound of spurs were jingling along the boardwalks. Hefty went to the local mercantile to pick up some supplies, while Lance tried his luck for information at the nearest dance hall.

It seemed the drovers they were looking to join had left town just yesterday. They had taken on supplies, enjoyed a store-bought meal, and spent the rest of the night gambling away their hard-earned wages and dancing with ladies of the night.

"The young lady stayed at the hotel until they were hitched up and ready to move out," the bartender said.

"They had a lady with them?" Lance asked.

"Sure did. Cute as a cub coon in a hollow log."

"What are they doing with a woman on a trip through this part of the country?" Lance asked.

"Her father is a colonel at Fort Griffin, Texas, and the government is paying a fee to have those cowboys get her to the fort."

Hefty, meanwhile, had filled out his list of needed supplies, and joined Lance in the dance hall and ordered a beer. Lance settled for a cup of coffee.

Lance said, "I got lucky with this depression coffee. I'm on the front end of it."

"I never heard of that brand of coffee," Hefty said.

"It's not a brand; it's a way of making it. The first of the week you put a pound of coffee in the pot. You add water to it for four or five days, each time it gets low. Monday's coffee would float a horseshoe. Friday's coffee is more like bathwater. Today must be Monday."

"It's Tuesday; you missed the best coffee by one day," replied the bartender as he walked by.

"We best hit leather if we expect to meet up with the drovers and the woman," Lance said.

"Woman? What woman?" Hefty asked.

"I'll explain it on the way."

"Seein' as how we burned the better part of today, we just as well might treat ourselves to a meal at the hotel," Hefty said.

"Good idea," Lance replied.

As they walked over to the hotel restaurant Lance filled Hefty in on what he had found out about the wranglers and the lady that accompanied them. Lance selected a table that allowed him full view of the room and the door.

The bar was a makeshift building constructed from whatever its builders could get their hands on. Towns like Baxter Springs just seemed to sprout up wherever someone thought they could make a quick buck and move on. Most of the men in the restaurant part of the hotel were ranchers, drovers, and buffalo hunters. The smell in the room reflected the clientele. Several of the tables had poker games going. The majority of the customers were discussing the events of the day.

"What'll you have, gents?" asked the waiter.

Lance said, "Make mine the biggest steak you have, and just cook it so's you hurt it enough it won't get better."

Hefty said, "Make mine the same."

The waiter soon returned with steaks hanging over both ends of a long plate, a steamy pot of beans, and a loaf of freshly made bread.

They both ate like they hadn't eaten in a week. That wasn't far from the truth when they considered what they had been living on. They were washing down the last bite of bread with some strong coffee as the bartender came to the table with the tab.

"You boys just passing through?" he asked.

"Yep, headed for Fort Griffin, Texas," replied Lance.

"We are?" Hefty said.

"I found out that's where the drovers are going, and I think we best tag along," Lance said.

"Haven't been there myself, but from what I hear, since the buffalo hunting has fallen off, a lot of the hunters have turned to easy money, mostly thieving and stock stealing. Best keep a close watch on your belongin's and your hides," the bartender said.

"Seems the closer we get to Texas, the less friendly it gets," Hefty said.

"I'm sure you'll win them over when we get there," Lance replied.

Their money was running too low to consider sleeping the night in the hotel, so they set up a dry camp just south of town on the banks of Spring Creek, and turned in to prepare for an early start come daylight. They should have guessed from the swirling, muddy, high creek full of debris that it was raining up north.

CHAPTER 5

Sometime during the night it began to rain, it rained and rained. It was a real cob floater. Come morning, Lance struggled to build a fire and cook up some breakfast under the tarp they had rigged up the night before. The rain showed no sign of letting up.

"We can travel wet just as well as sit here wet, so we just as well head out," Lance said.

After hurrying through a damp breakfast, they saddled up, loaded their belongings, and headed south. Once they got in the saddle and put on their oiled-down dusters they were able to keep reasonably dry. The day was uneventful, which was the way they preferred it, since they were in Indian Territory. The plains had given way to rolling hills covered with knee-high sedge grass, buffalo grass, and wildflowers. Just before dark, the rain let up and they spotted smoke from the wet wood burning in a campfire. A mile later they approached the drover's camp.

"Hello the camp," shouted Lance.

"Welcome. Come in and dry out your bones," replied one of the men around the fire.

"I'm Lance and this here's Hefty," Lance said.

"Jake Furnace," replied the man, who rose to meet them. He was about six feet tall, and had blonde hair and steel-blue eyes that looked right through you. He was solid muscle, broad shouldered, and long legged for his height. "Me and the boys here are headed for Fort Griffin, Texas, after delivering a mixed herd to Kansas City."

"Hefty and I have been trying to meet up with you. Figure there's a little more safety in numbers. We heard in Baxter Springs that you were headed for Fort Griffin and would like to join you, if you're agreeable to that."

"You have business at Fort Griffin?" Jake asked.

"No sir, actually we are headed for Bell County, Texas. We hear there is plenty of land there at a good price. We plan to try our hand at ranching."

"Fort Griffin is about a hundred miles out of your way, but I'm sure if you get to Griffin, you can connect with some folks, military or civilian, headed for Fort Worth. That will put you within spittin' distance of Bell County. I'm the trail boss of this motley crew. I'm responsible for getting us up and back safely. If you have no problems following my directions, you're welcome to join us. We can always use a couple of extra hands. As you can guess, we lost some of the men to the big-city life back in Kansas City. I figure they will be heading back when their money runs out."

Lance took an immediate liking to Jake. The trail boss struck him as a man not afraid to make decisions and tough enough to stick with what he believed. Lance decided he was one to walk the river with. He was certainly one that Lance would like to have on his side in a scrap.

"You have a deal, and we will be glad to pay for the grub," Lance replied.

"No need for that. You'll earn your keep and then some."

Jake noticed Lance eyeing a large tent that was all buttoned up with a lamp burning inside. "One thing you need to know. We've been commissioned to get Colonel Scott's daughter, Miss Amy, to the fort safe and sound. She is to be treated with respect, and is to be assisted in whatever way need be to accomplish that mission. Any problems with that?"

"No sir," Lance said.

"And you, Hefty?"

"No problem, Jake."

Jake shook hands with Hefty, then Lance. Lance felt the power of Jake's handshake and noticed his rough hands, the result of hard ranch work.

Lance and Hefty made the rounds and introduced themselves to the drovers. There were twelve, not counting Jake. They all seemed like decent enough folks and none of them asked any personal questions. Hefty and Lance hoped the men would judge them on their worth during the trip, and not on any baggage they brought with them.

Jake took Lance and Hefty to Amy Scott's tent for introductions. Amy stepped out of the tent when she heard Jake's voice, and walked toward the three men.

"Miss Scott, this is Lance and Hefty. They will be joining us for the remainder of our trip to the fort."

"Very pleased to meet you gentlemen; do call me Amy."

Amy was a striking young lady in her early twenties, the likes of which were not often found on the trail. She stood about five foot six, with auburn hair and deep blue eyes. She was a buxom lass, slim of hip, with skin that showed little evidence of exposure to the harsh southwest sun and dry air. It took Lance a few seconds to collect himself after first seeing her.

"The pleasure is all mine," stammered Lance.

"Likewise," echoed Hefty.

"I will try to be as little burden as possible," she said.

"You'll be no burden at all," replied Lance. He wondered if he might need to take that statement back after he got to know her some. He couldn't imagine any burden too big for such a fetching lady.

But then, he knew less about ladies than Hefty, and that wasn't much.

"Will you be staying at Fort Griffin?" Amy asked.

"No ma'am, Hefty and I will be going on to Bell County."

"If you should need anything for your trip out of the fort, I will be glad to speak to my father on your behalf."

"Much obliged, ma'am," replied Lance.

The cook, named Vittles, asked them if they had eaten. When they acknowledged they hadn't, he fixed them a plate of beef stew, hot biscuits, and sorghum.

Hefty said, "I believe I'm going to enjoy this leg of our trek."

Lance and Hefty took their plates and moved off a little from the others to eat.

"I think that filly took a shine to you," Hefty said.

"You're talking through that ten-gallon hat you bought at Baxter Springs," Lance said. "You sure didn't have much to say to the young lady."

"I told you, I have no truck with females, especially ones that are near as tall as I am," Hefty replied.

As they finished their meals, Lance could not get the sight of Amy out of his mind. She was a fine-looking woman. He had to remind himself that maybe he already had a wife, perhaps children. Then his mind began to wander over the same old questions: Who was his father, and what of his mother? Did he even have a mother? Hefty had said the letters were only from his father. Letter writing was usually delegated to mothers. Was his father a rancher, a business man, a soldier, or an outlaw, for that matter? And what of his wild recurring dream where everyone around him was in Confederate uniforms, but they were images of him. As he turned in for the night, hoping not to dream again, Lance decided he could not allow himself to have any feelings for the ladies until he knew more about himself.

CHAPTER 6

They woke up before dawn to the smell of coffee cooking. Vittles served them scrambled eggs, side meat, pancakes, and all the coffee they could drink. The cowboys had camped on the north side of Spavinaw Creek in hopes that it would recede by the next day, when they would have to cross it. But morning showed the river to be as high, if not a little higher, than it was the day before. The rains had the water spilling over its banks, and the current was dangerously swift.

Some of Jake's men scouted the river to find the best place to cross. They found a spot to get the horses across. The water was not more than shoulder deep on the animals. They had enough practice on the drive north to know the horses could swim across, reaching the far side downstream. The wagons posed the problem. Their sideboards would present considerable resistance to the rushing current and would cause them to flip. A plan had to be devised to keep the wagons right side up.

There were quite a few oak trees in the area, and Lance suggested that they fell four of them and lash them to the sides of the wagons to give them bottom-side weight. Vittles came up with two axes that he had stored in the wagon coonie. Lance and Hefty were no strangers to taking down trees. In short order they had four good-sized timbers down and cleared of limbs. Johnny and Sam, two of the cowboys, tied them to each side of the two wagons. Four cowboys crossed the creek on horseback, letting out ropes as they crossed. They tied these ropes to trees on the far side of the creek. With the ropes now tied fast to the trees on both sides of the creek at water level, four more cowboys began escorting the chuck wagon across the river. The ropes were on the downstream side of the wagon to prevent drifting during the crossing.

One cowboy lost his offside stirrup about midstream. He was swept out of the saddle, but managed to grab the horn and hold on while his horse made his way to the far bank. The four horses hitched to the chuck wagon pulled hard against their rigging. Vittles knew his wagon and the horses pulling it. He kept them moving, and made steady progress until they climbed out of the water on the far side. The jury-rigging they did with the logs and ropes was working fine. Now it was time to move Amy's wagon across.

"I'd be glad too drive your wagon across," Lance said.

"Thank you, but I'm sure I'll be alright. I've had a lot of practice with this rig the past few days."

Lance could see by the look on her face that her words spoke of more confidence than she possessed.

"Yes ma'am. I'll be right behind you if you should need any help."

Lance admired her independence and gumption, but worried about her judgment. She entered the water with her wagon, with four cowboys in the lead and Lance and Hefty bringing up the rear. She was making good progress, when she heard Johnny on the far shore yell out, "Trouble upstream!"

Lance looked upstream in time to see a huge cottonwood tree, uprooted by the storm, rushing down toward Amy's wagon. She was distracted by the sight long enough to allow her horses to stop. The wagon bogged down and she was unable to get it moving again. In seconds the tree would be at the wagon.

Lance spurred Bess. He moved alongside the wagon next to where Amy was seated. He reached out, snatched her from the seat, rolled back his horse, and headed to the near shore. He had just cleared the rear of the wagon when the tree slammed into it. The force snapped the ropes and flipped the wagon, sending it drifting. Lance made it safely to shore with Amy and lowered her to the ground.

Hefty was on the upstream side of the wagon. He turned his horse and moved toward the two horses that were still in the harness. There was enough slack in the chains to release them. He cut lines, which were caught up in the wagon, letting the horses drift free to make their way to the far shore.

"Are you okay, ma'am?" Lance asked.

"I think so," Amy replied, obviously shaken. "I've lost my wagon and all my goods."

"Yes ma'am, but you saved your hide."

"*You* saved my hide, Mr.—Mr.—"

"Just 'Lance' will do fine."

Hefty had moved on across and now returned to Lance with a spare horse, and they helped a wet and embarrassed Amy mount up. It was obvious she had never forked a horse before. Most women rode sidesaddle, particularly if they were from the northeast. She felt awkward in that long, wet cotton dress, but she knew there was no other choice.

The three of them entered the river, with Amy between Lance and Hefty. Several times the current almost got the best of Amy, but Lance and Hefty kept her in the saddle. When everyone was safe on the south side of the river, Jake decided to take a day to dry out and regroup. He figured Amy needed the time to collect herself and find some dry clothes to wear. Being the only female on the trip, she would have to make do with clothes from some of the cowboys.

Jake singled out Hefty and two other men who were short, and asked them to come up with a change of clothes for Amy. The cowboys had stowed some clothes in the chuck wagon, and were able to come up with enough for her. Lance and Hefty were traveling light, but Hefty did contribute a shirt she could wear. Her tent was lost as well, so she would be sleeping in the open air from here on in. It was still over two hundred miles to Fort Griffin, which meant a dozen more days on the trail, even under the best conditions.

Later that evening the boys rounded up a stray beef and the crew sat down to steak, pinto beans, and biscuits. Amy walked up to where Lance and Hefty were finishing their coffee and said, "I can't thank you enough for all you did for me and the horses during that crossing. I guess I should have let you drive the wagon, Lance."

Lance's face flushed as he removed his hat.

"That wagon would have been lost no matter who was driving it," Lance replied, shaking his head. "I'm just glad you weren't hurt."

"Just the same, I owe my safe crossing to you. Your wife must feel very lucky to have you as a husband."

Lanced broke eye contact with Amy and cleared his throat as he tried to think of a reply.

"Oh, he doesn't have a wife. No time for courtin' with the war and all," Hefty said.

Amy looked at Lance, waiting for a response. He glanced at Hefty, but said nothing. After a moment, Amy smiled with a twinkle in her eye, wished them good night, then turned and walked toward the fire the men were building. Once she was far enough away not to hear, Lance said, "You must know something I don't."

"Well, my guess is as good as yours," Hefty replied. Lance just shook his head.

By morning they were dried out and ready to ride. Lance couldn't help noticing how fetching Amy looked in her cowboy duds. But then, he decided she'd make a gunnysack look good.

In the afternoon the weather cleared and the ground dried out. They were making good time, and the streams they had to cross were no challenge compared to what they had just experienced. Their travel to the southwest was putting them into Comanche and Apache territory. Jake kept two riders out front and two in the rear to keep a lookout for any sign of trouble. Indians were their main concern, but outlaws were becoming more commonplace since the end of the war.

Amy proved to be a fast learner and a real trooper when it came to trail smarts. She also began to look downright at home in that western saddle. She had no trouble going the distance on each day's ride. With her father being a career army man, she had been raised around firearms, and during one of their target practices, she proved to be a good shot with a rifle and a revolver. Lance figured the drovers cut some of their practices short because Amy was out-shooting about half of them.

The boys were great trail hands, but none of them could call themselves gunmen. One evening after setting up camp, Hefty was taking bets that no one in the camp could outshoot Lance. Lance was not happy with the attention drawn to him, but there was no stopping Hefty. Vittles set out a half dozen empty bean tins at twenty paces. Since Lance (prodded by Hefty) was the challenger, he would shoot last.

Six cowboys and Jake decided to compete. Each one took a full cylinder of cartridges and emptied them at the cans. After taking a slow and steady aim, only Jake and one cowboy named Dace hit a can with five of the six rounds.

Now it was Lance's turn. His movement was smooth and quick as a cat as he drew and fired all six rounds without any visible aiming. All six cans went tumbling across the ground with a loud "ping" and flying dust. The cowboys stood staring, speechless. Lance dropped out the empties and nonchalantly refilled the cylinders with five cartridges, leaving the space under the hammer empty for safety. The long and short of it was, no one could hold a candle to Lance with a revolver, and he just edged out Jake with the rifle.

Hefty raked in about two months of the cowboys' pay.

That night, Lance lay awake wondering where he had developed such a skill. He had a natural feel for it, but the ability and speed he had must have come from a lot of target practice, or something worse. He was getting very anxious to learn about his past, and at the same time, afraid of what he might discover. He could be a wanted man. That was even more reason not to use his real last name.

CHAPTER 7

T he weather held and travel was good for the next week. As they approached the Washita River, they came upon fresh unshod pony tracks. There appeared to be ten to twelve riders not far off. Sure enough, shortly after crossing the river they spotted smoke from a campfire. Jake took Lance and moved in for a closer look. As they moved in under cover of a cottonwood grove, Lance whispered, "Looks like a Cherokee hunting party. No paint and no lookouts posted. They're not expecting any trouble."

"How did you come up with that? I thought you were never in this part of the country," Jake said.

The question caught Lance by surprise. "Ah

hell, you can just tell by looking," he replied.

"Well, I'm looking, and I didn't see all that," Jake said.

"I guess I just looked harder," Lance replied, but he wondered.

They returned to their camp and reported on what they had found. After some discussion, the group decided to proceed by skirting the hunting party while keeping an eye on their whereabouts. Hefty volunteered to be the lookout and follow the movement of the band until the drovers were out of the Cherokees' hunting grounds. They saw no more of the Cherokees, and when Hefty came back into camp at the end of the day, he announced that the band had moved off to the northeast.

As Amy walked up to the campfire, Jake said, "With luck we should be at Fort Griffin in four days, Miss Scott."

"I must say, it's been a great experience, but I'll be glad to reach the fort and see Father."

"You can be sure we're going to do our best to get you there safe and sound."

There was something in Jake's voice that gave Amy cause for concern, but she responded with a smile, turned, and walked back to the campfire.

Later that afternoon, she saw Lance over by the highline working on his horse's feet. She had been making a habit of visiting with Lance and Hefty over her last cup of coffee in the evening, so it was not unusual for her to approach Lance. She felt comfortable talking to Lance although he seemed a little uneasy interacting with her. He tended to be at a loss for words when she was around.

"Having a problem with your horse, Lance?" she asked.

"No ma'am," he replied as he straightened up and whipped off his hands, "Just resetting a shoe she loosened today."

"I notice you spend a lot of time with your horse. You must be very fond of her," she said.

"I'm not sure 'fond' is the right word. I have a lot of respect for Bess, and I consider her an important part of my survival. Without a good horse, a body is not likely to live long out here."

"Speaking of survival is there something I should know that Jake is not telling me?" she asked.

"I guess that depends on what he told you," Lance replied cautiously, his eyes still on Bess.

"He really didn't tell me anything. It was just the way he seemed to feel the need to assure me of my safety."

Lance was quiet for a moment, considering, then turned to face her. "Well, I guess you have as much right as the rest of us to know what we could be in for," he said. "Hefty was out hunting for game when he happened on some buffalo hunters who warned him about possible trouble with the Apaches. It seems they're spoilin' for a fight. For the last year or so they've been driven west out of their hunting grounds by the Comanche, and now the white man is killing off all their buffalo. They took their revenge out on a couple of merchant wagons headed for Santa Fe. Killed four of the men, and left one wishin' he was dead. Not likely they will try to take us on, but you never know what they have in mind until they make their move. If you don't plan ahead, oftentimes it's too late."

"Maybe they won't even discover us before we get out of their territory," Amy said hopefully.

"According to Hefty, it's a little late for that. He came across barefoot pony tracks that cut our trail about two miles back."

"Is there anything we can do?" Amy asked.

"It's already been done. Jake sent Dace ahead to Fort Griffin to request a military escort. It's not likely they can spare the troops, but Jake figures we are moving a precious cargo that could swing a decision in our favor."

"Father will not jeopardize the safety of the fort."

"I'm sure that's true ma'am, but he could get very creative on how to protect the fort and you."

"If there's a way, Father will find it. He has a lot of experience handling problems with the Indians."

"Well we can hope for the best and be prepared for the worst and maybe we can come out somewhere in between. I'd appreciate it if you would not make yourself conspicuous. It wouldn't help to advertise that we have a lady among us."

"I'll do my best. With the men's clothes and this hat I have a good chance of just looking like "one of the boys".

"I wouldn't say that ma'am but it's a start. Take care ma'am."

Lance felt the blood rush to his face as he turned and returned to the men.

CHAPTER 8

It was just at sunset when Dace reached the fort. He hailed the guard, identified himself, and asked to see Colonel Scott. He informed the colonel of the situation with his daughter and the cowboys, and estimated that they were about two days from the fort. Colonel Scott was a tall man and stood erect before Dace. He had close-set gray eyes and a thick crop of auburn hair, and his years in the sun gave him a ruddy complexion that made him look older than his forty-five years. He had a reputation for being a no-nonsense graduate of the Point, and one to follow military orders. Nevertheless, his solemn face with its angular features and prominent nose betrayed concern for his daughter's safety. He

paced the floor of his office for several minutes before replying to Dace's report. His eyes falling on a
small portrait of his daughter he kept on his desk,
Colonel Scott could not help but be reminded of her
mother's likeness. She had died of the fever five
years earlier. His chin set, he turned, looked at
Dace, and asked, "How many Apaches are in the
party?"

"About fifteen, near as one of our men could
guess."

"I have scarcely enough troops to tend to the
problems with the Comanche in this sector. My first
obligation is the safety of this fort and its troops, but
perhaps I could spare twenty men under the command of Lieutenant Bascom, if they leave the fort in
darkness. With no moon we may be able to make
the move without detection. It would not be good to
have it known that we're short on defenses for the
fort. Can you find your way back, at least for the
first day, traveling at night?"

"Kinda thought that could come up. I did a good
job of checking the looks of my back trail. Getting
back in the dark will be the least of our problems,"
Dace replied.

"Get something to eat at the mess hall and try to
catch some sleep, and be ready to leave at midnight," Colonel Scott said.

The colonel had selected Lieutenant Bascom
because he was the most experienced platoon leader
in routing Comanches who were threatening settlers
in the area. He also knew that the lieutenant had met

Amy and taken a shine to her when he was serving under him in his last assignment at Fort Belknap. Colonel Scott thought that might give Lieutenant Bascom a little additional motivation to get the group back safely.

Dace was saddled up and ready to ride when the orderly came by to wake him at eleven thirty. He was eager to get back to his friends with the support that could mean the difference between life and death. Dace introduced himself to Bascom, and gave him a briefing of the route they would be taking to meet up with the wranglers.

Word was passed from man to man to move out. Keeping a low profile, the troops walked the horses out of the fort and to the stand of cottonwood trees to the north. At that point they mounted up and followed Dace's lead. The going was slow following each other by sound rather than sight.

"It's darker than the inside of a cow," Dace said to Lieutenant Bascom.

"Get used to it, Dace; we won't see a hint of daylight for another six hours. How is Miss Scott?" the lieutenant asked after a moment.

"Last time I saw her, she was perky as a filly on a frosty Friday," Dace replied. He detected by the silence that followed that he may have gotten a little too personal for the lieutenant's druthers.

By daylight, they were almost twenty miles northeast of the fort. The weather was clear and the ground dry. They could expect to reach Amy and the wranglers in another day, based on their pace and the expected progress of Jake's crew.

At sunup they came upon a small stream. Lieutenant Bascom called for a halt and a break long enough to let the horses blow and for the men to take on some grub. Some of the troops took advantage of the off time to catch a little sleep. Dace scouted ahead to see if there was any sign of traffic on the trail. He came upon his own tracks made on the way to the fort, but no sign of any company. He reported back to the lieutenant that the way was clear ahead, but he suggested that they may want to use a forward observer from here on. The Texas hill country was the kind of terrain that provided good opportunity for an ambush by Indians or bandits. Their horses and weapons would make good trading items for either of the unwanted parties. The lieutenant called for the men to mount up, and assigned one of them to stay a half mile ahead of the main body.

It was daylight now, and Dace's tracks from the incoming trip made the route easy to follow. About noon, the trooper who was scouting ahead returned to the detachment and reported that he had spotted ten cowboys headed north on the trail ahead of them. They were driving a mixed herd of about three hundred cows. Since the troopers were making better time than the wranglers, they would be overtaking them by mid- afternoon. Lieutenant Bascom explained the situation to his unit, and told them to mind their manners as they came upon the cowboys. He cautioned them not to do anything that would cause the cattle to stampede. As they approached the herd, the cowboy that appeared to be the trail boss turned back to meet them. The lieutenant introduced himself and explained that they were headed northeast on a military mission.

The trail boss did not have the appearance of a typical wrangler. He wore his revolver low on his leg, and the holster was lashed to his leg. He wore a fine pair of form-fitting gloves. All the other cowboys were armed as well. That surprised Dace, since most trail bosses would have the men put up their revolvers to prevent any accidental firing that could excite the cattle.

"The name's John, John Hardin," the trail boss said. "We're taking our herd to the railhead up north of here." Hardin was civil, but by no means friendly. He appeared annoyed with this unexpected company. Dace noticed that Hardin was paying particular attention to all the troops and their weapons. Hardin did not look at people; he studied them. His dark mustache and deep-set eyes gave him a sinister look. He was not a man to be taken lightly.

Dace also thought it strange that such a small herd should have so many different brands. Hardin caught Dace's stare, rolled his horse back to face him, and said, "Somethin' bothering you, cowboy?"

The cold steel look of the man made the hair stand on the back of Dace's neck.

"No sir, nothing at all," he replied.

Dace had no doubt that he was facing a man who was looking for trouble. If he didn't find it, he would probably create it when he could. Since Dace didn't take the bait, Hardin turned his attention back to the lieutenant and said, "Unless you think you have business with me, I'll be tending to my herd."

"Our business is elsewhere for now, but perhaps we'll meet again in the near future."

"Anytime, it will be my pleasure. See you around, cowboy," Hardin said, as he threw a glance at Dace.

As Bascom and his men moved out ahead of the herd, the lieutenant motioned for Dace to ride alongside him

"Do you know who that was, Dace?"

"I guess he was who he said he was, John Hardin," Dace replied.

"John Wesley Hardin, to be exact," replied Bascom.

"Is that supposed to mean something to me?" asked Dace.

"It should, if you care to live a little longer. He has a reputation as a hothead with a hair trigger. He's already killed one man, and he's not but a teenager," Bascom said.

"Did he have good cause?" asked Dace.

"Said he shot him because he wouldn't stop snoring; you be the judge."

"I guess it's a good thing I didn't breathe too loud," Dace said.

"I'm sure he's wanted. If it wasn't for my orders, I would have taken him to the state authorities," Bascom said.

"That may not have been as easy as it sounds. I think he kind 'a figured that's what you had in mind. I believe he was even looking forward to you trying," Dace said.

"His turn will come in due time," said Bascom.

Dace was pleased with himself. His instincts had told him Hardin was no stranger to trouble. As it turned out, they would both live to see another day.

CHAPTER 9

Jake figured Dace would bring the troops, if they were coming, on the same trail Dace had taken out. He made sure they stayed on that trail as they moved southwest to Fort Griffin. Jake had no way of knowing the troops and Dace were only a day and a half away.

It was midmorning when they appeared on the horizon. There must have been near two dozen of them. They were Apaches, and well armed, wearing paint.

"I don't think they plan to stop by for tea, Jake," Lance said.

Lance borrowed Jake's binoculars and studied the band carefully. There was something about their leader that caught his attention. He wasn't sure what it was.

"Jake, I think we best be looking for a place to hold up, make a stand, and hope that Dace is on his way with help," Lance said.

"I agree, and that cottonwood brake up ahead is as good as any place," Jake replied.

They moved on at a steady pace as the warriors moved parallel to them. When they reached the brake, they made a run for it. It took the Indians by surprise, and it was a few seconds before they could react. That was just the time they needed to reach the trees.

Amy kept her head and followed Jake's directions to stay in the middle of the group. Everyone dismounted, and Vittles took charge of the horses. The cowboys used the trees and the chuck wagon for protection. They took Amy well behind their defense line, where she would be safe for the time being. The Indians held their position.

Lance took a handgun from his saddlebag and gave it to Amy. "I know you know how to use one of these," he said to her.

Amy was trying to put up a good front and not show her fear. She hesitated a few seconds before accepting the handgun.

"My father saw to it that I learned how to handle revolvers and rifles, she said as her voice trembled.

"Good! You may get a chance to put your practice to use. Shootin' people is not the same as shootin' tins. Don't think; just shoot if you need to."

"Lance, how much trouble are we in?" she asked, as Lance turned to walk away.

"We can hold them off for a while and we can hope that Dace is on his way with the soldiers from the fort."

Lance was being a bit overoptimistic for Amy's benefit, and he hoped she didn't see through it. The Indians were well-armed, seasoned fighters. The cowboys' position needed to be defended on three sides, and that left them a little short on manpower. Lance knew their only hope would be help from the fort.

Lance returned to Jake, and borrowed his binoculars once more to study the Indians' leader. Lance could not get shed of the feeling that somehow he had a connection to this young brave.

"Jake, if they come at us from several sides, we won't be able to hold them off," Lance said as he lowered the glasses.

"We will have to do the best we can. I don't see that we have any choice," Jake replied. "We must not let them take Miss Scott. Can I count on you to see that doesn't happen?"

Lance shot a look at Jake, hesitated, then replied, "You can count on it Jake; they won't take her alive."

Lance stood looking out toward the Indians, rubbing his chin with his left hand, then turned to Jake and said, "There is one other possibility."

"And just what is that?" Jake replied.

"I could go out and talk with them, maybe strike a deal."

"That's called suicide. They are in paint and looking for trouble. We have nothing to deal with."

"Look, we are dead men anyway, so what is there to lose by letting me try? Besides, I can't explain it, but I just have a feeling that I can work something out," Lance said.

"It's your hide; I won't try to stop you if you're set on it. At the very least, it might buy us some time."

Lance nodded, then went to Hefty and told him what he had in mind. He told him what he had to do for Amy if they were being overrun. "If I don't make it, you can have my outfit. See that Miss Scott does not fall into their hands. If you can get on to Belton, look up my father and tell him what happened. Don't get the wrong idea. I'm not looking to get myself killed. I can't explain it, but I just have a feeling this will work out."

Lance collected up his horse from Vittles, and was checking his rigging when Amy approached him.

"You shouldn't be here, Amy," Lance said.

"I heard what you plan on doing. Couldn't we just wait for the soldiers to get here?"

Lance shook his head. "There's no tellin' how long they will be, and we sure can't count on the Indians to wait for them," he replied.

"I'm not sure why, but I feel like you'll be successful with them. I hope I'm right. May God be with you, Lance."

"I'm not sure He would want any part of me,

but thanks for the thought. I can use all the help I can get."

"Amy, I know it must seem like I have been avoiding you on this trip, but I have my reasons." Lance said awkwardly.

"Yes, I know." Amy broke in; "Hefty told me about your loss of memory and your concern about your past and your possible family obligations."

"Hefty always talks too much," Lance said.

"It's a good thing he does. I wouldn't know anything about you if he didn't."

"I just want you to know, well, that I care about you. If we get through this situation, and I get the loose ends of my past figured out, I'd like to call on you, if you would allow me."

"I'd like that very much, Lance."

Their eyes met and for an instant Lance was tempted to take her in his arms, but he thought better of it. It was not the time or place, he thought. Amy leaned up and kissed him on the cheek, and said, "Come back safely."

Lance turned away from her, stepped into the stirrup, and swung into the saddle.

"See ya 'round," Lance said as he coaxed Bess to the edge of the tree line.

He tied a white handkerchief to the end of his rifle barrel, held it up in plain view, and moved out toward the band of Indians.

CHAPTER 10

As he approached the Indians, one warrior raised his rifle and aimed it at Lance. But the man who appeared to be their leader pushed the rifle aside and uttered something to the one holding the rifle. The leader was staring intently at Lance. As Lance closed the distance between them, he studied the band to determine where the earliest and most serious threat may arise. As he approached them, he had decided which brave he must take out first to have a chance to survive.

Lance pulled up just a few feet from the leader, who sat proud and erect on the multicolored blanket he had draped over his large sorrel stallion. His skin looked like boot leather that had been left out in the rain. He was so lean that every muscle in his body stood out, a testimony to his strength. He wore only a loincloth with a large knife at his waist and a U.S. Army muzzle-loading rifle across his horse's withers.

Before Lance could speak, the man said, "It has been many moons since we last met, Kincaid."

Lance tried his best to hide his surprise, deciding it would not do to try and explain his situation. He replied as though he remembered the brave, "Yes, it has," and he tensed, waiting for the other man's response, hoping for a clue to guide his own actions.

The leader looked at his warriors and spoke to them in Apache, then turned toward Lance, urging his sorrel alongside Lance's mare. The warrior took hold of Lance's right hand, pulled it toward him, and pushed up Lance's shirtsleeve. He pointed to a long straight scar on the underside of Lance's forearm. The warriors all took note of the scar as their leader repeated what he had just said to them. It was a scar that Lance had assumed was a result of his injuries in the war. Lance looked from the scar on his arm to a matching scar on the forearm of the Indian leader, his mind racing. Where had he known this Indian, and why did they share the same scar?

"What brings my blood brother to this place?" the leader asked.

Blood brother! So that was it. Apparently he had done something to gain the respect of this leader, and the Indian had made him a blood brother. Lance decided to play out his hand and hope for the best. It would be a challenge, since he didn't even know the cards he was holding, let alone the play that the Indians were planning.

"We have the responsibility of delivering a young lady to her father at Fort Griffin," Lance replied. He did not think it would be to his advantage to let the Indians know she was the fort commander's daughter. He added, "I ask that you grant us safe passage so that we may be able to complete our journey."

"The Great Spirit tests us in strange ways. You saved our women and children from death at the hands of your white brothers; now it is my time to spare your life. Many things have changed since you escorted us to the white man's fort. Your father in Washington promised us food and blankets and land that we could use to grow crops. The food was not fit to eat. The blankets never came. The land was not good enough to grow locoweed. We had no choice but to leave the reservation. Today we are hunted by your yellow leg soldiers.

"I am sorry it has come to this," replied Lance. "I wish I had the power with my people to make it different. I, like you, believed in the promises of the reservation. It is not my government that does this injustice to you and your people. It is the evil people who have been put in charge of your welfare. I promise I will do all I can to see that the men doing wrong will be punished, and the proper people be put in charge."

"It is too late, Kincaid. We are now called criminals and savages. We are hunted down by your outlaws, your yellow legs, your ranchers, and the Comanches. They show no mercy as they kill our women and children. You saved us from being massacred by your star. I see no star now, and it is beyond your power. Once we were many and now we are few. Before long there will be no more Lipan forever."

The Indian's words went racing through Lance's mind. He had a star. Was he a sheriff, a marshal, or maybe even a Texas Ranger? He tried to put these questions out of his mind and pay attention to the challenge at hand. He believed the Indian, and from what he had read and heard, it was a fairly accurate account of what the Indians were suffering. There were three thousand Lipan Apaches when they were moved to Fort Belknap. Now the tribe was less than two hundred. Lance truly felt for the plight of the Indians, and he meant what he said to this leader. He also knew there was little chance he could make a difference. He asked himself which he would choose, to return to the reservation to starve, or to die fighting for his freedom. Neither choice had much to offer.

Before he could speak, the Indian said, "I know you have a true heart, and I believe you remain my blood brother. I will allow you to travel unharmed by my warriors, but I cannot speak for others of our people. If you come upon them on your journey, tell them you are blood brother to Two Ponies—that may save your life. Do not tell the Comanche you are a brother to the Lipan; they will take pleasure in killing you. Go in peace, brother. I wish you well. Let us hope we will meet again in better times."

Lance shared the sorrow that he heard in Two Ponies' voice. The Indian's shoulders slowly sagged from the burden he carried. The two men looked long and hard into each other's eyes. Lance reached out and took Two Ponies' hand. Even though he could not remember their past encounter, he felt that he had just spent time with a true and caring friend. He asked himself, just who were the savages, and who the civilized?

Lance could think of no more to say. "Until we meet again," he said as he turned slowly back to the trees.

A moment later, he looked over his shoulder to the ridge where Two Ponies had been. The ridge was empty. It was unlikely that he would ever see this trusted friend again. The way things seemed to be going, there would soon be no more Lipans.

Hefty came running up to him as Lance reached the tree line.

"What in tarnation happened out there?"

"Just had a visit with an old friend," Lance replied.

As the others gathered around him, he recounted the incident to the men and to Amy. He told them they were probably safe as far as Apaches were concerned, but that they were fair game for the Commanches. When he finished, Jake had the men mount up and move out to meet up with the cavalry detachment. His best guess was that Dace and the soldiers should be within a day's ride—that is, if they were coming.

CHAPTER 11

They made ten more miles before setting up camp for the night. Vittles had the cowboys gather up wood for a fire. He cooked up beef stew in a giant iron kettle suspended over the fire, and baked a couple dozen sourdough biscuits. There was also all the steaming coffee you could drink in a large porcelain-coated pot perched on a rock next to the fire.

After asking permission to join her, Lance shared the sitting space of a fallen cottonwood trunk with Amy while they ate their dinner.

"That was a brave thing you did today," Amy said as Lance sat down.

"It doesn't take a lot of courage to talk with an

old friend," he replied.

She shook her head. "You didn't know he was a friend. I thought it was the end of you when I saw that brave raise his rifle."

"That makes two of us," Lance admitted. "I just wish things were different, so that I could have asked Two Ponies some questions to try and jog my memory. It's truly worrisome to not have any recollection of my past. There is not an hour that I don't trouble myself over my identity. I'm still plagued with a dream in which Hefty is cutting me down with a saber on the battlefield. And why was I wearing a Johnny Reb uniform in that dream? Could I have switched sides during the war? It seems I am from Texas. How could I have ended up in the Union Army?"

Amy replied, "I haven't known you long, Lance, but I know you well enough to believe that you could never fight on the side of slavery. It has little to do with where you are from. It's your moral values and your respect for others that dictates your character. I saw a true sense of sorrow in your manner when you returned from your meeting with those Indians. Even with your loss of memory, you felt camaraderie with that Indian leader before you met with him. I think you wanted to meet with him to save him from harm, just as well as us."

Lance sighed. "I'd like to believe that, Amy, but I really can't be sure right now. Two Ponies said I used to wear a star. That's a step in the right direction, except there are a lot of star-toting renegades out here that hide their foul deeds behind a title or symbol of fair play and justice."

"You're not one of them, Lance. I'd bet my life on that."

Lance thanked her for her vote of confidence, and the two finished their meal in silence. Finally Lance rose and excused himself to return to the men. He had to force himself to leave her side. His attraction for her grew by the hour. He constantly reminded himself that it was not fair to become attached to her until he had the answers to a lot of questions about himself. But he couldn't help feeling she would be one to walk the river with, if a man could be lucky enough to win her over. Perhaps the day would come for him.

As the evening grew dark, Jake posted four guards, and the camp settled in. At midnight, they were relieved by a second shift. The night was uneventful except for a pack of coyotes that howled from midnight 'til dawn.

By noon the next day, they met up with Dace and the military detachment. Greetings were exchanged, and Jake described their brief encounter with the Lipan Apaches.

"You are very lucky Mr. Kincaid," the Lieutenant said. "The Lipans have very little to gain being civil to the whites. If they are off the reservation they are considered renegades and our orders are to destroy them." He then turned his attention to Amy. Lance could not help but notice his interest, and eyed them a bit anxiously.

It was obvious, however, that Lieutenant Bascom was much more excited at seeing Amy than she was at seeing him. She was polite and considerate of his effort to escort them to the fort, but her demeanor was cool and reserved.

"Your father sends his love and concern for your safe arrival to the fort. He regrets that he was not able to personally escort you in," Bascom said.

"It has been too long since I have seen Father, and it will be good to be with him again. I would not expect him to jeopardize the safety the fort or the area ranchers by leaving his command to hold my hand on the way," Amy replied.

After an uncomfortable pause, the lieutenant turned to Jake. "I suggest we take advantage of what light we have left and move on toward the fort, Mr. Furnace. We will be out two nights before we reach the fort, if all goes well."

"Lead the way, Lieutenant," replied Jake.

As they moved out, Hefty rode alongside Lance and said, "You know, Lance, you win a lady's favor by accident easier than I do on purpose."

"What is that supposed to mean?" Lance replied.

"Miss Amy was quite taken with your Indian powwow. Did I ever tell you about the time I tried to impress my date one night back in Pennsylvania?"

"No, but I expect I'm going to hear about it now," replied Lance.

"Well, sir, my pappy and I were hunting squirrel

one fall when we came across a possum. Pa said, 'Let me show you how to catch a possum.' He walked up close to it and shook out a handkerchief in front of it with his left hand. Once he had the possum's attention on the kerchief, he reached down with his right hand, grabbed it by the tail, and lifted him straight up off the ground. That possum was not strong enough to roll up and bite Pa's hand, so Pa had him a possum by the tail."

"What does that have to do with winning over ladies?" Lance asked.

"I'm getting to that. About a month later, I was taking my date for an evening buggy ride when I spotted a raccoon crossing the road. My lantern caused the raccoon to freeze in his tracks. That raccoon was about the same size and shape as a possum, and he moved about like them. So, I said to my date, 'Do you want to see how ya' catch a raccoon?' Before she could even answer, I jumped out of the buggy with the lantern still holding the raccoon's attention; I worked my way around the back of the raccoon, grabbed that fuzzy tail, and lifted him off the ground. In the bat of an eye, that raccoon turned up and clamped onto my hand. I let out a yell and let go of the tail, and he let go of me. I can tell you my date was not too impressed as she took the reins and drove me to the doctor to have my hand tended to. I never did tell Pa that I learned an important difference between a possum and a raccoon. Like I say, I have no truck with females."

"I think I know why," Lance laughed.

"You, on the other hand, just won over that little Miss Amy's heart," Hefty said.

"I'm not so sure about that. I believe the lieutenant is kind of sweet on Amy. Apparently they know each other from the past," Lance replied.

"I guarantee you, the feeling is not mutual. He couldn't hold a shuck to you when it comes to her feelings. She sure was in a world of hurt when you headed out for your meetin' with the Lipans."

"Did I ever tell you, you talk too much, Hefty?"

"You may have mentioned it once or twice."

Lance rolled his mare back and moved along the column until he came alongside Lieutenant Bascom. "If you don't mind, Lieutenant, I'd like to do a little scouting along our flank."

"Don't mind at all, Mr. Kincaid. Just make sure you stay within sight of our column. I don't want to send any of our men looking for you."

"Understand. I'll be in before dark."

Lance turned his mare and set an easy lope to reach a course about two hundred yards west of and parallel to the column. He wanted to make sure they didn't have any unwanted neighbors, but more importantly, he wanted time alone. Each day he became more and more concerned about the things he didn't know about himself. He was also having a difficult time keeping his feelings for Amy under control.

For the next day and a half, things went off without a hitch. Lance rode the flank watch during the day, and spent most of his camp time with

Hefty. As they approached within ten miles of Fort Griffin, Lance, riding the west flank, noticed a column of smoke about a half mile west of their route. He reported his sighting to Jake and the lieutenant.

"I'm familiar with this area, Jake, and it sounds like the direction of the Nelsons' ranch," the lieutenant said. "Jed Nelson has a small spread just northwest of the fort. I have stopped by to check on them several times when we were concerned about Indian attacks."

"It looks like it's time to check on them again," Lance replied.

"That's not possible," Lieutenant Bascom said. "My orders are to escort Jake's crew and Miss Scott to the fort. I can't afford to place any of you in harm's way. Perhaps I can check on the Nelsons after I get you safely to the fort."

"I'm afraid that may be too late," Lance replied. "Hefty and I are not officially a part of Jake's crew. We could take a look-see without jeopardizing your orders. That is, if Hefty would like to join me."

"Count me in, Lance," Hefty shouted.

"I can't prevent you from making that decision, but you have to realize, if trouble arises, I won't be able to send any help for you until we reach the fort late today."

"Yes sir, I understand that. If all goes well, we will catch up with you before you reach the fort."

Hefty and Lance packed a few supplies and their bedrolls, filled their canteens, and stepped into their saddles.

Amy came up alongside Lance, reached up, and took his hand. "Please be careful, Lance. Don't take any foolish chances."

Lance felt Bascom's eyes on him, and knew that Amy's gesture had not gone unnoticed by the lieutenant.

"Don't worry," Lance said lightly. "I'll have Hefty to keep me out of trouble. If we get in any tight spots, Hefty will just talk our way out of it. We'll see you before you get to the fort."

CHAPTER 12

Lance and Hefty turned their mounts to the west and lit out at an easy gallop. Both men checked the loads in their handguns and rifles. The smoke was still rising, and they heard sporadic gunshots from that direction. They moved across a wide wash and gave their horses their heads to climb the last rise, which looked down on the ranch house.

As they topped the rise, they saw a dozen or so Indians on horseback firing into the house. The barn was in flames and about to collapse. Without a word, Hefty jumped from his horse, took up his Hawkins, set the sights for four hundred yards, and squeezed off a round that blew one of the Indians off his mount. By that time Lance had fired a couple of shots. The attacking Indians, taken by surprise, weren't sure how many were firing at them. They let out a couple of blood-curdling yells and took off to the west. Hefty swung back into the saddle and was about to race to the ranch house. Lance reached up and grabbed his reins.

"We're not going to do any good by getting ourselves killed. Let's make sure it's safe to move in."

Lance had no sooner gotten the words out when two more Indians ran out of the ranch house. Both were armed with rifles. One took aim and fired a shot that put a hole in Hefty's chaps. Hefty and Lance dove for the ground. Before they could get off a shot, the two Indians were on the other side of the ranch house, mounted, and galloping west. After about ten seconds, Lance said, "I'll move to the house. Keep me covered."

"You got it," Hefty replied.

Lance reached the house without incident. As he entered the front door he found a man and woman dead on the dirt floor near the window. They had several arrows in them. He heard a noise from the back room and froze. The door to that room had several large holes in it that had been made by the two braves trying to get at whoever was inside. He also noticed two holes that looked like bullet holes made from the inside. Lance loudly identified himself as a friend and asked them to come out. The door slowly opened, and a boy of no more than twelve stood in the doorway holding a rifle. At the sight of his parents he let out a scream, and fell across the body of his mother.

Hefty entered the house, and he and Lance did what they could to console the boy. The boy pushed back from his mother, stood up, and wiped his eyes, but he continued to stare at his parents as if unable to move. After a moment, Hefty took the boy outside, and asked him to sit on the bench that was by the front door.

"They ran off our cattle and horses, then they killed my folks. Why did they have to kill my folks?"

Before Hefty could work up an answer, Lance came to the door. "There's something strange about this attack," he said.

"Well, I hope it wasn't your friend Two Ponies that did this," Hefty replied grimly.

"It wasn't. It wasn't even Indians."

"What are you talking about? I saw them. I even shot one."

"Those folks have arrows in them, but the Indians we saw had rifles. I think you better go check the Indian you shot."

Hefty went to the rider on the ground, and rolled him over on his back. "Well, I'll be! This is no Indian. It's a white man dressed like an Indian with some sort of dye on his skin."

"That's what I figured. These are renegades looking for a way to get rid of Indians and make some easy money while they're at it. They steal livestock and herd them over to the Western, Chisholm, or Old Shawnee trails. They sell them off to any trail boss who isn't too particular about brands. They make it look like Indians are to blame so the soldiers or vigilantes have an excuse to hunt them down and kill them. Not that they need any excuse, with General Sheridan calling for their extinction."

Hefty swore beneath his breath. "What do you think we should do?"

"We need to get these folks buried proper, and convince that youngster to go to the fort with us. We'll take the body of that imposter back as proof the Indians did not commit this act. Maybe someone at the fort will recognize him. That could lead to the other culprits."

They were able to round up the horse that belonged to the scoundrel. It was only fitting that his own horse should carry him to the fort.

The boy sat motionless next to the bodies of his mother and father while Lance and Hefty dug the graves. The lad never said a word as his fallen tears dampened the dusty soil. Lance sat down beside the boy, put his arm around him, and tried to comfort him. The boy did not respond. After some urging on Lance's part, the boy finally released the grip he had on his mother's hand, and stood up. They convinced him that his only choice was to go to Fort Griffin, where he could be looked after.

Hefty stayed behind to bury the bodies, and Lance headed out with the boy to meet the others. He moved out in a direction that would prevent the boy the pain of seeing his parents being lowered into the ground.

Hefty caught up with them just before they met up with the main party, about three miles north of the fort. Lance explained to Jake and Lieutenant Bascom what had happened to the Nelsons. The lieutenant approached the body draped over the horse, grabbed the dead man's hair, and pulled his head up. "I know this man. He and several others were 'stinkers' for Ed Jones and Joe Plummer until the buffalo herds got too small to keep them busy."

"What do you mean, 'stinkers?" Lance asked.

"That's what we call buffalo skinners at the fort, because of the way they smell," Bascom replied. "Colonel Scott will be very glad to hear about this. He has suspected for some time that the Indians were getting a bad rap, but until now he couldn't prove it. We have a very difficult situation here in west Texas. Soldiers returned from the war and couldn't find work. Many of them became buffalo hunters. Some were very successful, like Jones and Plummer."

"They had acres of hides drying at a time, Jake said. " They used the trace to haul the hides north so often that it became a cattle trace known as the Western Trail. It was not unusual to have as many as two hundred thousand hides shipped to the East in a year."

"Problem is the herds are thinning out. Unless something is done to curtail the hunting, there won't be any buffalo left in a few years," Dace added

Jake shook his head. "It's not likely that anything will be done, since Sheridan wants all the buffalo killed as a way to starve the Indians."

"The Indians starve all right; then they steal cattle from the ranchers to get enough to eat," the lieutenant added. "But the lack of buffalo also means lack of work for the skinners. Unfortunately, some of those hunters turned to outlawing, and some of the ranchers hire the outlaws to kill the Indians. It's hard to figure a solution to this mess."

"It looks like the Indians are going to go the way of the buffalo," Lance said.

"I'm afraid you may be right, Lance," the lieutenant said. "The Indians are being put upon by the army, the Texas Rangers, the drovers, and each other".

Lance looked at the lieutenant and said, "They can't survive long under these conditions. I hear the politicians in Washington believe in a thing called 'Manifest Destiny.' That's what they use to justify the invasion of Indian Territory by the white man. I don't hold with that kind of thinking. I guess I don't understand politics much."

Lance turned back on the column and joined Hefty, who was checking on Amy. Hefty had filled Amy in on what he and Lance had experienced.

"I'm glad you are back safely, Lance," Amy said as Lance approached them.

"I'm afraid we didn't get to the Nelsons in time to do them much good. We did get their boy out of harm's way," Lance replied.

Jake had followed Lance, and overhearing him, said, "You have done more than you realize. That body we are taking in may just be enough evidence to allow Colonel Scott to hunt down and hang the culprits that have been responsible for a number of killings. No tellin' how many more they have in mind."

Lance appreciated the input, but he still felt lower than a snake's belly, thinking about Mr. and Mrs. Nelson and their son being left without parents. Jake suggested that the boy ride next to Amy. She was happy to have him with her. She could see that he was in a state of shock and disbelief. She put her arm around him and pulled him to her. He exhibited no reaction.

"What's your name son," she asked.

The boy showed no acknowledgement of the question. He continued to look straight ahead with no life in is eyes.

"Would you like to stay with Colonel Scott and me at the fort?"

No Reaction.

"I know you have just been through a terrible experience and nothing anyone can do will bring back your folks. I'm sure if they were here the one thing they would not want you to do would be to ruin your life because of their deaths. They have a chance to live on through you. You don't want to disappoint them do you?"

The boy looked up at Amy and said, "But why did those men kill my ma and pa? They never did nothin' to them."

"They are bad men and they will be caught and

punished. One of them is already dead and Colonel Scott will see that the others are caught."

"If Colonel doesn't catch them I promise one day I will. --- My name is Buck ma'am."

"My name is Amy, Buck. I think you and I are going to become good friends."

Little Buck broke down and began to sob. Amy leaned down and kissed him on the forehead. There was not much else she could say or do for the time being. At least she got him to open up and let out some of his emotions. They headed for the fort.

CHAPTER 13

Where there was a collection of soldiers and many transients due to nearby cattle trails, it was not unusual to find a settlement. Fort Griffin was no exception. As they approached the Clear Fork of the Brazos River, they could hear the sounds of the town of Fort Griffin. The town, known as "The Flat," was located below the post on the banks of the river. The main street was alive with wagons, horses, and people. Building material was stacked everywhere, and men were busy constructing new buildings to add to the stores, dance halls, livery stables, and hotels that catered to soldiers, ranchers, buffalo hunters, and thirsty drovers that came in off the Western Cattle Trail, which passed just to the west. The town had its share of outlaws and professional gamblers. It was obvious that the main pastimes were gambling, drinking, and the companionship of prostitutes. Lance noticed Hefty taking in the entire goings-on with a hungry eye. He couldn't help but wonder if Hefty would be ready to move on as quickly as Lance had planned.

As they crossed the river, they passed by the prostitutes' cribs, the blacksmith shop, the hotel, and a little farther down the street, the Beehive Saloon. The locals paid them very little attention as they passed by the merchants of the town. Patrols were not an unusual sight, and even the covered body on the horse being led seemed to go unnoticed. As they passed by the last hotel and started up the hill to the fort, Lance noticed an Indian camp to the west on the banks of what he later found to be Collins Creek.

The fort, originally called Camp Wilson, had recently been renamed Fort Griffin in honor of the late General Charles Griffin. The fort was just south of the river on a bluff that allowed full view of the plains to the west and north. It had no walls or gates, and was not built to withstand siege warfare. It was a place from which campaigns could be initiated, and a retreat where soldiers could recuperate and mend from their encounters out on the plains with the Comanches. The personnel consisted of four companies of the Sixth Cavalry, serving under Colonel Scott, and a band of Tonkawa Indians serving as scouts, living just to the north at the junction of Collins Creek and the Clear Fork. It was the responsibility of the troops to protect the settlers and travelers in the area. This post was also expected to be a key supply source for the Red River campaigns planned for the near future. Their ultimate goal for the fort was the removal of the raiding Kiowa and Comanche warriors from West Texas. Since the hostile Indians in the area were not well organized and only traveled in groups of a dozen or less, they were no threat to the fort. But their random guerrilla raiding techniques made it very difficult for the soldiers to maintain the peace. It was not unusual for whites in the area to meet with misfortune before the soldiers could come to their rescue.

As the group reached the top of the hill, Lance surveyed their destination with interest. The fort consisted of six buildings of stone and another ninety or so picket huts built of vertical logs with earth and canvas roofs. There were four rows of barracks, nine each eight-by-thirteen-foot frame buildings in each row, with wood floors and a fireplace in each building. In a pinch, each hut could house six men. Two men per hut was a more livable arrangement.

Several units were drilling on the parade grounds as they moved along the east side of the grounds to reach the commanding officer's quarters. A posted guard had recognized the unit approaching the fort, and sent word to the commander. Colonel Scott was on the north veranda of his quarters watching for their arrival. At first he did not recognize his daughter in the distance. He had never seen her in cowboy clothes, including a wide-brim western hat. Once he saw her, however, he flew to her side, bypassed military procedure, helped her down from her horse, and greeted her with a long, tender embrace and a kiss on the cheek. Amy and her father exchanged warm words as they looked lovingly into each other's eyes.

The colonel then tried to regain control of his emotions after this uncharacteristic display in front of his troops, but Lance noticed the hint of a tear in the corner of his eye. Colonel Scott collected himself and called for his orderly to escort Amy to the room he had prepared for her in his quarters. He then returned to military protocol and invited the lieutenant and Jake to his headquarters for a full report of the mission. Lance, Hefty, and the cowboys were shown to the stables, where they unsaddled their horses, brushed them down, and gave them some grass hay and a ration of oats. A first sergeant showed them to the barracks, where there were enough beds to house them during their stay. After the body of the buffalo hunter was identified, it was taken to the hospital to be prepared for burial.

Jake returned to the barracks after his visit with Colonel Scott, and told Lance that he was invited to join the colonel and his daughter for dinner that evening at the colonel's quarters. Lance was more interested in getting off to Bell County in the morning, but he felt an obligation to accept the offer. Besides, it would give him an opportunity to see Amy once more before he left the fort.

"The boys and I will be leaving for the Bell

County area in a few days," Jake added. "They will need a little time at The Flat to let off a little steam. You and Hefty are welcome to join us."

"Thank you for the offer, but I don't want to take any more time than necessary to get on to Bell County. Hefty and I will be getting off first thing in the morning."

"I kind of figured you'd say that, knowing your situation. I guess getting the right answers would give you a clear shot at Miss Scott."

"It seems to me you and Hefty are looking to get me roped into a romance."

"You could do a lot worse, Lance; besides, she's kind of sweet on you, much to Lieutenant Bascom's disappointment."

"There's a lot of ground to cover and a lot of answers to be found before I can give romance any priority in my life."

"Just remember, it never hurts to keep an oar in, Lance, especially if you're in friendly waters," Jake said, clapping him on the shoulder.

"I'll keep that in mind, Jake."

Lance washed up and was putting on a clean shirt when Hefty walked up and asked him what the occasion was that warranted all the sprucing up.

"I've been invited to Colonel Scott's quarters for dinner tonight," Lance replied, avoiding eye contact.

"And I know who did the inviting," Hefty said, with a sly grin on his face.

"Now, don't you start; I assume the colonel did

the inviting, and don't you assume otherwise. Hefty, you can make more out of nothing than anybody I ever met."

"I just call it the way I see it."

"Well, then, I think you better get you a pair of spectacles. I plan to be back early and pack up the supplies we need for our trip. Be ready to leave at first light—that is, if you still plan to go with me."

"Oh, I plan to go with you. I wouldn't want to miss all the excitement you seem to create wherever you go."

"I hate to disappoint you, but I don't plan to create any excitement."

"You won't need to plan it," Hefty said as he turned and walked back to his bunk.

Lance ran his fingers through his thick wavy hair and wiped his boots off on the back of his pant legs before he knocked on the colonel's door.

"Lance, we haven't formally met; I'm Colonel Scott. I feel as though I already know you. I have heard a lot about you from Jake and my daughter Amy."

Lanced felt his face flush a little as he shot a quick glance at Amy, then turned back to the colonel and said, "Pleased to meet you, sir. I want to thank you for the dinner invitation."

"You're certainly welcome. After Amy told me all you did for her on the trip, it's the least I can do to show my appreciation. Please sit down. Can I get you something to drink, a brandy perhaps?"

"No thank you, sir. I'm not much of a drinkin' man."

"Very well, dinner will be ready shortly. My mess sergeant is a great cook. He has prepared some roast beef with all the trimmings."

"Will you be staying long at the fort, Lance?" Amy asked.

"No ma'am, Hefty and I will be pulling out in the morning."

The disappointment showed on Amy's face as she said, "I'm sorry to hear that, but I appreciate that you have things to attend to elsewhere."

"Amy told me about your loss of memory. Are you making any progress in your recall?" the colonel asked.

"I'm sorry to say I'm not, sir. I only have a recurring dream that includes Hefty and me in a Confederate uniform, which makes no sense at all. The only other scrap of information is when the Indian, Two Ponies, recognized me from a previous meeting and referred to a star I was wearing. That hasn't filled in many blanks. I'm hoping all that will change when I get back and meet up with my father in Bell County."

The mess sergeant announced dinner, and they took their seats at a large rough-cut oak table. They enjoyed the beef along with sourdough biscuits, beans, and gravy, and a dessert of peach cobbler made from the local peaches. During the meal Colonel Scott asked Lance about his trip from Illinois, and whether he had had any trouble from Confederates. Lance told him of the run-in he had with the Yankee in the wagon train.

"I advise you to be careful with your Union leanings in the part of the country you're headed," the colonel told him. "There are still strong Confederate feelings in Texas, and I'm sorry to say there are injustices being done by the federal government's representatives that only aggravate those sentiments. You'd best see which way the wind is blowing before you take any strong stands."

"I thought as much," Lance nodded.

"Are any of the wranglers leaving with you?" the colonel asked.

"No sir. I guess they need a few days to 'let off steam' at The Flat. There's no tellin' how long that will take."

Colonel Scott put down his coffee cup and looked at Lance seriously. "We have been having a considerable amount of trouble with Comanche war parties to our east. I ask that you delay your departure one day to allow me to arrange for one of the Tonkawa scouts to accompany you to Bell County. They know the country, and more important, they know the mind of the Comanche. It won't do you much good to leave the fort early if you don't make the trip safely."

"I would appreciate the support, sir. I'm afraid I'm not in a good position to pay you for the services of a scout, but I'm sure he could make the trip a lot easier for my partner Hefty and me. Besides, I know Hefty would just as soon have an evening at The Flat."

"Let's just say the use of the scout is payment

for you bringing in the "stinker" that was posing as an Indian raider. I plan to track down and arrest the remainder of those troublemakers. Your action will result in saving the lives of many settlers, not to mention their livestock. I'll have a scout ready to join you at daybreak day after tomorrow."

"Thank you, sir."

Colonel Scott glanced over at Amy and said, "I have army business to see to, so I will be bidding you good evening. Don't let me rush you, Lance. I'm sure Amy will be glad to visit with you while you finish your coffee."

Amy tried to hold back the blush in her cheeks. She smiled at her father and said, "Thank you, Father, I'll be along shortly."

The colonel excused himself and retired to his office to attend to the business of the fort.

There was a moment of silence at the table as Lance took his time finishing his coffee. Amy could see that Lance was at a loss for words. She watched as he fussed with his cup and avoided eye contact with her. She decided that he had suffered enough and broke the silence.

"Father likes you. He is very discriminating when it comes to my friends. You must have made a very favorable impression on him. I certainly agree with him. I will miss you, Lance."

Lance looked up from his cup and the blush on his face showed uneasiness with what he was about to say.

"I have grown fonder of you than I have any

right to, Amy. I can't ask you to wait for me until I get my life together, but if things work out, I plan to come back and call on you, if it's not too late. I can see that Lieutenant Bascom has taken a shine to you, and I can't blame you if you return his attention."

"Lieutenant Bascom is a fine young man, but he can never be more than a friend. I have given him no reason to think otherwise. I'm in no hurry to find my life's partner. I will look forward to hearing from you when you reach Bell County."

As Lance rose from the table he said, "It won't be soon enough for me."

Lance was moving slowly toward the door as Amy left the table to join him. He took her hand and kissed her gently on the cheek. She returned the gesture by getting up on her toes and kissing him on the lips. He held her in his arms and drowned himself in the smell of her perfume. That tender kiss and her warm soft lips aroused a passion he didn't know he had in him. It was all he could do to tear himself away.

"Good night, Amy."

Lance didn't look back as he turned and went out the door.

"Be careful and hurry back safely," Amy called out as he disappeared into the darkness of the parade ground.

CHAPTER 14

Hefty was cleaning his rifle when Lance entered the barracks. He looked up at Lance and said, "I can tell by that fire burning in your eyes, you had a very enjoyable dinner with the colonel. I don't suppose Miss Scott joined the two of you."

"Don't start that again or I won't give you the good news. Leastways, good news for you."

"You found me a female companion for the evening," Hefty said with a grin from ear to ear.

"No, but maybe you could find your own. We are not leaving in the morning. Colonel Scott has offered to provide us with a guide for our trip east. He'll make the arrangements, and we'll leave with the scout at daylight the day after tomorrow. That means you can go on into The Flat and partake of what social life it has to offer the likes of you."

"That is good news! It's been a long time since I've been to a real live town. Why don't you join me? I'll buy you a beer. That is, if you think Miss Scott would approve," he teased.

"You are just lucky I am loaded with tolerance when it comes to your smart remarks. You go on ahead. I have some work to do on my saddle. I'll be along shortly and take you up on your offer. Meet you in an hour or so at the Beehive Saloon."

"That's a deal."

Lance set about to cut new rawhide tie-downs for his saddle. He had used the old ones to lash the body of the make-believe Comanche to the horse for transporting him to the fort. Once he completed that task he decided to clean his 44 revolver and his long gun. He finished up in less than an hour, and headed to The Flat for that beer he had coming.

He could hear the town long before he could see it. Apparently a cattle drive was holed up just two miles west of The Flat, and the boys had all come in for a night on the town. The dance halls were so full they had cowboys hanging out the windows. Lance looked around for the busiest house of entertainment. He figured that's where he would find Hefty. He didn't have to look long. As he approached the Beehive Saloon, the swinging doors flew open and Hefty came flying out on his back.

"What's going on?" Lance asked, as Hefty looked up at him.

"I'm having a slight disagreement with a gentleman as to just who won the war," Hefty replied.

Before Lance could say anything, Hefty was on his feet and at a dead run back into the saloon. Lance stepped through the doors to see a nasty-looking buffalo hunter squaring off on Hefty. The man was half again the size of Hefty, standing over six feet tall, and his broad shoulders were only matched by the belly that was hanging over his belt. He had a full red beard and hair down to his shoulders that looked like it hadn't been washed since Lee surrendered. Lance could smell him from across the room. The man's deep-set black eyes were focused on Hefty. He had two front teeth missing, and tobacco juice was running down his beard. His nose looked like it had ended up on the wrong end of a fist more than once.

"What's it going to take to convince you? Blue Coats ain't never going to take over the South," the man shouted.

"It's going to take more than you got, Johnnie Reb," Hefty replied.

Lance was tempted to close his eyes and miss what was coming next. It was a good thing he didn't. The buffalo hunter had a friend, who came up behind Hefty and locked both of Hefty's arms behind his back. The buffalo hunter was about lay into him when Lance stepped in and put the barrel of his 44 just behind the ear of the Hefty's captor.

"Throw that punch and your friend here is wolf meat," Lance said.

The man stopped his swing in mid-flight and

took one step back.

"What's your interest in this affair, pretty boy? Do you want a piece of this action?" the hunter said.

"No sir, I have no interest in politics. I just don't like to see a man playing against a stacked deck. I'd feel a lot better if your friend here would just free this little man's arms and stay out of the fracas."

The man released Hefty and Lance lowered his gun. At that moment the hunter let loose with a right hook that sent Hefty flying across the room and up against the bar. The big man moved in to finish the dance. He sent his huge right fist at Hefty's head. At the last second Hefty rolled to one side, and the fist slammed into the bar rail. That missed punch left the hunter's midsection wide open. Hefty stepped in and landed a right hook to the belly that took the wind out of the big guy. Then Hefty kicked him in the knee. The body blow and kick caused the hunter to double over. That put his face in just the right position for the uppercut that Hefty brought up from the floor. The big fella's eyes rolled back in his head, and he slowly came forward to the floor like a giant felled tree.

Lance looked at Hefty and could see he was still reeling from that last right hook.

"You better sit down before you fall down."

Hefty took his advice and plopped down in one of the chairs at a nearby table.

"He might whup me, but he is sure gonna know he's doin' it," Hefty mumbled.

"If he is gonna whip you he is gonna have to

come to first," Lance replied.

"Did I win?" Hefty said as he tried to focus.

"I'd say that's a fair assessment, but we best get out of here before we wear out our welcome."

Lance helped Hefty to his feet with his left hand, keeping his right hand free in case the hunter's friend had trouble in mind. They slowly backed their way to the swinging doors. It looked as though the buffalo hunters had had enough fun for one evening.

Hefty pulled himself into the saddle with considerable moaning and groaning. As Lance mounted, he suggested that the party was over and they should head for the fort. He got no argument from Hefty as they turned their horses up the street toward the hill that led to the fort. By the time they reached the stables, Hefty's head was clearing and the pain was setting in.

"Sorry to cause you all that trouble back in town," Hefty said, slurring his words through a swollen jaw.

"No need to apologize to me. You had all the trouble. I just lent a little moral support. But I think we will both do better from here on in if we keep our politics to ourselves."

"You got that right."

After tending to their horses, they headed for their barracks. Lance lay awake on his cot for several hours, listening to Hefty groan in his sleep, and trying to formulate a plan for his arrival in Bell County. He was beginning to believe, as he had been advised, there could be reason not to advertise his identity and purpose. The war was long past, but the bitterness between the North and South was intense. He decided that his first name would be enough to go by until he connected up with his father.

Lance spent the next day visiting with the soldiers who were not pulling duty. He tried to learn all he could about the area to the east. He asked about the trails, settlers, water sources, and Indians. He also asked about the Texas Rangers who might be in the vicinity of the fort. He learned that there was no love lost between the army and the Rangers. The missions of each were at odds with the other, and often caused friction. It was the army's responsibility to control and protect the Indians, while looking after the safety of the settlers. It was the Rangers' mission to remove the Indians from Texas, or kill those who refused to leave. The Rangers also had the responsibility of tracking down civilian criminals. The soldiers had no jurisdiction over most civilians, and were no help to the Rangers.

These were difficult times for everyone. The Plains Indians were hunters and gatherers with no permanent villages. They roamed the plains as nomads, moving with the availability of food and water. The settlers were moving west in search of new opportunities, trying to get away from the crowded industrialized East. The government was encouraging western migration with promises of land. When the government tried to protect parcels of land for the Indians, the migrating settlers ignored the borders and moved in on the Indians. The armies of the West were reluctant to arrest or deport families, and Lance doubted if they had the resources to do it even if they tried. It seemed from everything he heard that, right or wrong, the western movement and the fulfillment of Manifest Destiny were not going to be stopped. The only alternatives were the removal of the Indians, the corralling of the Indians on reservations, or their destruction.

Unfortunately, as he had learned from Two Ponies' plight, the reservation alternative often resulted in their destruction. Thousand of Indians were dying on the reservations because of lack of medical attention and inadequate food and shelter. Even if the reservation plan had worked, Lance wondered if Texas would ever allow any permanent Indian reservations in the state.

As if that were not enough to deal with, there was the issue of the freed slaves and the treatment of them by many of the whites. For the most part, they were "freed" with no money, no education, and no job. Many of them survived by joining the army. The "buffalo soldier" became a respected fighter and soldier.

Finally, there were the "carpetbaggers" and "scallywags" ready to step in and take advantage of a difficult situation in an effort to line their pockets with the Southerners' land and money. These were the worst of times for Texas.

All of these conditions reinforced Lance's decision to be careful in Bell County, not use his last name, and not express his political views. He again stressed his concerns with Hefty and advised him to keep his views to himself, at least for the time being.

Lance and Hefty were up before daylight on the morning they were to leave. They fed their horses and brushed them down, and Lance checked the shoes on his mare. They both were well aware that their lives could depend on their horses being in good condition. They were just beginning to saddle the horses when Colonel Scott's aide showed up accompanied by a tall, lean, solemn-looking Tonkawa Indian. As the aide approached Lance and Hefty he took a second look at Hefty's face.

"Looks like you made a visit to The Flats, cowboy. They say if you're goin' to dance you have to pay the fiddler. It looks like there was a pretty steep price for that dance."

"I look downright pretty compared to my dancing partner."

The aide just smiled as he stepped back to where the Indian that accompanied him was quietly standing.

"Gentlemen, this is your guide, Dark Moon. He will stay with you until you reach the Leon River at the north boundary of Bell County. He knows the route well, and knows the Kiowa even better."

Dark Moon stood silent as he was introduced. He showed no emotion or any acknowledgement of his introduction.

"I thought we were worried about the Comanche," Lance replied.

"That was last week. This week we have been told that Santanta, a young Kiowa chief, has been leaving the Oklahoma reservation near Fort Sill and raiding settlers and travelers in Texas. He recently signed a peace treaty with the United States, but he says the government has not met the agreements in the treaty. He has enlisted about forty braves to follow him on these raids into Texas. The Indian agent, a man by the name of Tom Bedford, has not been able to keep Santanta's raiding party on the reservation. This chief is outspoken, and freely admits to the raids. He claims he is only getting what has been promised him. It doesn't seem to bother him that he is killing settlers to get it."

"From what I have seen, he may be right, but that doesn't make me any more anxious to lose my scalp," replied Lance.

"I've grown kind of fond of mine over the years," Hefty said.

"That's why we have asked Dark Moon to join you. He has no love for the Kiowa. They killed his wife and son several years ago. He knows how they think, and can often anticipate their next moves. When it comes to tracking, Dark Moon is the best. He got his name because he can easily track by the dark of the moon." The aide paused, then added slowly, as if unsure how they would react, "He is considered to be a medicine man by his band. They claim his visions have saved many lives."

Lance nodded. "Dark Moon, I am Lance, and this is Hefty. We welcome you and thank you for joining us."

"I will see you safely to Bell County. Kiowa are fearless fighters, but they must find us before they can fight us. I will keep us hidden."

Lance noticed that Dark Moon was not armed except for a hunting knife, which he carried in a leather sheath in his waistband.

"Sergeant, would it be possible to get a long gun or revolver for Dark Moon?" he asked.

Before the sergeant could answer, Dark Moon said, "I'm not a warrior; I'm a farmer and medicine man. I will not need a gun."

Lance was surprised at Dark Moon's response. He wondered how safe he would be in the hands of a farmer. He hoped the medicine man half would make up for the farmer half.

Dark Moon was just under six feet tall, straight up and down from hips to shoulders, and carried himself erect. He was high waisted, with long arms for his height. There was no sign of body fat, and every muscle bulged through his golden skin. He wore his hair shoulder length, and was dressed in well-tanned leather. His sleeveless deerskin shirt was decorated in multicolored beads, with a fringe across his upper back. He wore a loincloth of leather with a beaded belt. His moccasins were mid-calf high and held in place with rawhide laces. A life exposed to the elements made it difficult to judge his age, but Lance thought mid-thirties would be a good guess.

Dark Moon's horse was a paint of fifteen hands, well muscled and certainly not overfed. The pony had no shoes, but appeared to have no need for them. He was fitted with makeshift stirrups that were attached by a cinch around his girth. A colorful Indian blanket served as a saddle. The horse's head was controlled by a rope bridle that passed through his mouth.

Dark Moon carried a leather pouch in which he had jerked buffalo and pemmican, in case he could not find enough to live off the land. He carried no water.

"Gentlemen, I wish you a safe journey," the sergeant said as he turned and walked back toward his barracks.

"Thank you, Sergeant. We'll do our best," Lance replied.

Lance and Hefty loaded the supplies into their saddlebags. They had beans, flour, bacon, jerked beef, and coffee. Each carried a hundred rounds of ammunition and a change of clothes.

"Packing up like this reminds me of the time I used a friend's mule as a packer to go deer hunting," Hefty began.

"And I'll bet I'm going to hear about it," Lance replied.

"Now that you asked . . . It was October in northern Pennsylvania, and I was going to take a city friend of mine deer hunting on horseback. He said he didn't know anything about horses. I told him not to worry; I knew enough for both of us. Well sir, I had a farmer friend by the name of Mance up near where we were going to hunt. He had a mule named Mousey he said was a good packer. I loaded all our supplies on that mule, including food, tent, ropes, and blankets, and secured them on old Mousey with a diamond hitch. I was riding and leading Mousey up the side of a mountain, and Mousey was following nose to tail. My friend was riding one of my horses bringing up the rear. As we topped that ridge, I heard a cowbell off in the distance. Then I heard it closer, and all of a sudden, Mousey pulled loose from me and headed on a dead run for that cowbell.

"It turned out that old Mance always kept a cowbell on one of his horses so he could locate the herd in the hills. Mousey recognized the ringing bell as one from Mance's herd, and decided to join them. I told my pilgrim friend to stay put while I retrieved the mule. Only problem was, my lariat was hanging on Mousey's pack. I got lucky, and while I was trying to run down old Mousey, my lariat fell off the pack. I stopped long enough to pick up the rope, and started out again as I was building a loop. That mule was a lot smarter than I gave him credit for. Somehow he knew I was not much of a roper. He heard me say, 'I've got to get our supplies. Either I rope this bugger or I'm going to shoot him dead.' Well sir, he stopped on the spot and stuck his head right through my loop. And that's the truth."

"I'll have to remember that if I need some roping done. I'll only ask you to rope animals that can read your mind," Lance replied.

After hearing the story, Dark Moon turned toward Lance with a perplexed look.

"Don't mind him, Dark Moon. He has more stories than a dog has fleas. And I'm sorry to say you'll be hearin' most of them. Let's mount up and move out. Lead the way, Dark Moon."

The trip to Bell County was over two hundred miles. Even averaging twenty-five miles a day it would be an eight-day ride. Lance decided that he would let Dark Moon not only lead the way, but also set the pace. The first day went without a hitch. They made almost thirty miles. The countryside was rolling hills and fields of knee-high grass. It was obvious where the near-surface water existed. Those areas had large brakes of live oaks, hackberry trees, and cottonwoods. Wildflowers, just beginning to bud out in the early spring, dotted the fields. As the sun set, the breezes caused the tall grass to sway and glisten like a golden ocean in the low light.

During the next two days they crossed several small canyons, some with water, some dry. The clouds threatened both days, but there was no rain. Dark Moon said very little, and stayed to himself when they camped at night. He did not accept Lance's offer to share their food. He did, however, accept some brewed coffee from them. After eating from his pouch he would move off alone and sit cross-legged for more than an hour, looking at the sky as if praying.

On the third day they were about to leave the wooded hill country and travel more on the plains. Dark Moon suggested that they camp early, take down a deer, and dry some meat to carry them through the next few days. After setting up camp, Hefty took his long gun and set out for the nearby hills to bring back a deer. He was not gone thirty minutes when Lance heard the crack of Hefty's gun.

Before long Hefty reappeared, leading his horse into camp with a deer draped across his saddle. "I've never seen so many deer," he said.

"Let's just hope there are not as many Kiowas. That cannon of yours can be heard for miles," Lance remarked.

"The Kiowa don't need to hear. They have seen us," Dark Moon said.

"I haven't seen any Indians," Hefty replied.

"I haven't either, but I sure had that feeling down my spine that we were being followed," Lance said.

"Two braves follow us for two days. They send one back to bring more braves. Will be a raiding party of ten, maybe twelve."

"I guess we better get prepared to make a stand," Hefty said.

"They can't fight if they can't find. We know where we go, they don't. Tonight we make good camp with big fire. There is no moon. By morning we will be fifteen miles away."

"I guess we will have to pass on jerking that deer meat, Hefty said.

"That is the least of our concerns for now," Lance replied. "What do you suggest Dark Moon?"

"We head southwest to river you call Palo Printo then through the foothills to the headwaters of the Leon River. Kiowa can't track like Dark Moon. We cover tracks to slow them down. Kiowa want easy kill, no want chase."

As had been their habit, they moved well out of the light of the fire to lay out the bedrolls. By nine o'clock it was darker than the inside of a cow. They quietly gathered up their gear, saddled, and left camp. The ground was sandy and soft. That helped keep down the noise that would have been made by the steel shoes on Lance's horse.

About two in the morning, Dark Moon stopped and motioned to Lance. Lance moved up alongside of Dark Moon and asked him what the problem was.

"No problem. Dark Moon need to check back trail. You soon come to river. Cross river and go south through canyon to beginning of Leon River. Follow river. No need horse, you take with you. Dark Moon join you soon."

He handed the rope bridle to Lance and disappeared into the darkness without a sound. Lance took up Dark Moon's horse, softly whispered for Hefty to follow him, and headed off in the direction Dark Moon had indicated. By daylight they had crossed the Palo Printo River and were well into the foothills to the south.

"I don't see hide nor hair of the Kiowa or our

scout," Hefty said softly.

"I don't expect to see any Kiowa, but I figure we'll be seein' Dark Moon any time now," Lance replied.

They decided they had put enough distance between them and the Kiowa and they could afford to stop for breakfast. They cooked up some bacon and beans, and had some cooked venison left over from yesterday. Just as they finished the last of the coffee, Dark Moon came walking into camp.

"Kiowa no problem. Braves no talk to raiding party." As he spoke he reached to his waistband and pulled up two scalps.

Lance took a deep breath and tried not to overreact to such a gruesome sight.

"We go now, soon reach your Bell County."

As Lance and Hefty readied their mounts, Hefty looked over to Lance and said, "I'm sure glad I finished breakfast before Dark Moon showed up with his souvenirs."

As they swung into the saddle, Lance thought about all the hatred and revenge that filled the air between tribes and between the tribes and the whites. Clearly, these emotions provided no solution to the problems they faced. But what was the solution? Where would it ever end? It seemed to Lance that the vengeance, fighting, and injustice had become so much the nature of man that it would take generations to undo the damage. Certainly it was not new. Such injustice had existed since biblical times. As difficult as it seemed, Lance knew he must focus, for the time being, on solving his own problems and not dwell on larger problems he could do nothing about. The best he could hope to do was to try to appreciate all sides of any situation, so that, if given an opportunity to make a difference, his action would be based on knowledge and not emotion.

Few words were exchanged as they rode through the rolling hills and through the stands of hackberry trees. Just before noon they reached the headwaters of South Nolan Creek. Dark Moon pulled up and turned to Lance.

"I leave now. Follow stream east and you reach town of Belton in your Bell County." He paused, and then added, "Kincaid, I think you troubled with bad dream that has no meaning to you. Meaning will come with time, but spirits tell me, your father is not part of answer. In my vision, I do not see your father. You are not welcome here, but you will receive help to see you through. Move with care, Kincaid. The Great Spirit protects the brave and just."

With that, Dark Moon turned his mount westward and rode out of sight. Lance was so taken by Dark Moon's remarks; he could not find the words for thanks or parting.

Hefty had sat silently and watched the exchange between the two.

"I like ol' Dark Moon, but he gives me the creeps. I always thought he was looking into my soul. Reminds me of the time I visited one of them palm readers on a dare by some of my army buddies. At first the visit went as I expected, with a lot of general statements that could pertain to most people. Then she said, 'You like to hunt big game.' That didn't seem too darn difficult to predict, since most men hunt. All of a sudden she got this strange look, like she was seeing ghosts, and she said, 'But you like to hunt different than others. I see no gun on your hunts, no bullets. Now I see it; you hunt with a bow.' Let me tell you that got my attention. I don't know to this day how she knew I hunted with a bow. But I do remember that look, and it was the same look I saw in Dark Moon's eyes."

"I didn't know you were good with the bow. That could come in handy," Lance said.

"You missed the whole point of my story. I'm trying to tell you there are some strange folks walking this earth of ours. I suggest you take Dark Moon's words to heart and pay close attention to the goings-on around you in this Bell County that you are so set on visiting."

"Oh, I plan to do just that," Lance said. "I agree there are a lot of things that we are not able to understand or explain with hard facts. Maybe this is one of them. I do believe there are those with an uncanny ability to sense, feel, or see events that lay ahead of us. I have had some reservations myself for the last few weeks concerning what I am going to face on this search."

With that, Lance urged his horse along the banks of South Nolan Creek toward Belton. This was west Bell County. It consisted of rolling hills deeply cut by streams and valleys. There were occasional rugged bluffs that rose some two hundred feet above the rolling plains. Cattle could be seen feeding on the tall sedge grass. A few ranch houses stood near some of the many springs. The fields were sprinkled with beautiful wildflowers— bluebonnets, verbena, daisies, Indian paintbrush, and others. Lance could see this was great ranching country, and a beautiful place for a person to call home. He couldn't help but wonder what Amy would think of this land.

Before long they were approaching the outskirts of Belton. As in many towns of its time, all the commercial activity was located on the square around the courthouse. Nolan Creek flowed just west of the square. As they entered the town, Lance spotted a brake of large hackberry trees near the streambed southwest of the courthouse. At his suggestion, they decided to set up camp in the shade of those trees. The site provided cover, water for the horses, and plenty of knee-high sedge grass for them to feed on.

Both men unsaddled their horses, brushed them down with bundles of grass, and led them to the stream to drink. Hefty put up a highline that they could use to keep the horses secure at night. They picketed the horses in the tall grass while they finished setting up camp and cleaned up at the stream. It was near sunset, and Lance decided to wait for morning to make any formal inquiries. He noticed that most of the night life was located on the east side of the square, and he figured that would be the place to get some local information and get the "lay of the land."

After putting their horses on the highline, they walked the short distance to the hotel on the west side of the square. The main room was a combined eatery and saloon. It hung heavy with cigar smoke, and there was the usual smell of beer in the air. The back wall was taken up by a carved hardwood bar with a brass foot rail and a large spittoon sitting on the floor at either end. The mirror behind the bar was framed with the decorative hardwood the bar was cut from. Large paintings of scantily clad ladies hung on the two side walls. As they made their way to an empty place at the bar, Lance noticed the crowd appeared to be people from all walks of life: merchants, bankers, farmers, ranchers, the local no-accounts, and drifters. The groups were pretty much segregated according to appearance. Lance and Hefty fit in with the eclectic group, and drew no special attention as they took their place at the bar.

Lance ordered his usual beer, and Hefty ordered whiskey with a beer chaser. Lance asked the bartender if they were serving dinner. The bartender replied that the special that night was wild turkey with all the trimmings. He added that the turkey was so fresh, it had been feeding on rye grass seed that afternoon.

"Sounds good to me," Lance said. "We have been eating on the trail so long that an old saddle cooked enough would taste good."

"Just get into town?" the bartender asked.

"Yep, came down from Fort Griffin with a message for a man thought to live in Bell County, if we can find him."

"I know a lot of folks hereabouts. Who is this man? Maybe I can help you locate him," the bartender replied.

"Rancher by the name of Kincaid."

The bartender stopped cleaning the glass he was working on and looked first at Lance, then at Hefty. After a few seconds of silence he said, "Can't say as I have ever heard the name. I think you may be looking in the wrong county."

"You sure could be right. I guess we will ask around a little in the morning and see if we can get a lead on him, but I appreciate your help."

As the bartender moved on to a customer at the other end of the bar, Hefty whispered to Lance, "Did you see his reaction when you said 'Kincaid'?"

"Yeah, I saw it, and I don't like what I saw."

Lance and Hefty took their drinks to an empty table and began looking over the menu. A young lady approached the table and said, "I see you're fixed for drinks. Will you be ordering some dinner?"

"That turkey the barkeep told us about sounds pretty good to me. How about you, Hefty?"

"Make it two, and a pot of strong coffee."

"You got it," she replied as she headed for the kitchen.

As they were working on their drinks, a man

approached their table. He was well dressed with a day's growth of beard, and appeared to be unarmed. Lance took in his large frame and his catlike movement. He walked light on his feet, as if he could move in any direction at a moment's notice. "My name is Bull Turner," he said as his held out his meat hook of a hand to Lance.

"I go by Lance."

The man seemed to be waiting for a last name. When he didn't get one, he said, "I understand you have a message for Kincaid."

"That I do. Do you know where I can find him?"

"Not just now, but he stops in here occasionally. I'd be glad to give him the message when I see him."

"Thanks, but I have been asked to give him the message personally."

"You'll likely have a long wait. There's no tellin' when he'll be through these parts again."

"We have no plans for moving on. When you see him, I'd appreciate it if you could look me up. We are camped at the hackberry brake just southwest of here."

The man shot a glance to Hefty, then to Lance with his wide-set dark eyes, shrugged his huge shoulders, turned, and walked back to the bar. Hefty watched him grimly. "If there is a fight, I hope that one is on our side. He looks like he could whip his weight in catamounts."

"I have a feeling we'll not be that lucky," Lance replied.

As they ate their meal, Lance turned over the recent events in his mind, deliberating. Finally he put down his silverware, looked at Hefty, and he said, "Hefty, I have that feeling on the back of my neck. I think things may get a little testy from here on in. You are far away from your 'Regulator' concerns. There's really no need for you to stay hooked up with me any longer. I'd have no hard feelings if you decided to go your own way."

"I didn't come all this way to miss the dance. Besides, Dark Moon said someone would lend you a hand. That might be me, and I wouldn't want to spoil his vision."

"Suit yourself, but if you change your mind, I'll understand."

After finishing the last of the coffee, they returned to their camp. Lance decided he'd visit the courthouse in the morning to see if he could locate any records of his father's ranch. He'd learned enough at the bar to be convinced his father was, or had been, in this area.

Lance had the coffee ready the next morning when Hefty tumbled out of his bedroll. There was a chill in the air that reminded them that spring hadn't really set in yet. Hefty fried up some side meat, and they had some of yesterday's biscuits. The hours dragged as Lance waited for the courthouse to open. Lance had spotted Payne's Mercantile in the square the night before, and he asked Hefty to get a needed stock of supplies while he visited the courthouse.

At nine o'clock, Lance headed for the courthouse, and Hefty readied his horse for the short trip to the supply store. The clerk greeted Lance as he entered the courthouse.

"May I help you?" he asked.

"I am trying to locate a Mr. Kincaid. Do you have any information that could help me find him?"

The name Kincaid obviously struck a note with the clerk. He nervously cleared his throat and asked, "What is your business with this Mr. Kincaid?"

"I have a message for him from Fort Griffin."

"Please wait here and I'll check our records to see if we have a Kincaid in our deed or tax records."

The clerk disappeared to a back room, and a few minutes later another gentleman emerged from the back and walked up to Lance.

"Good morning, sir, I am Judge Christian. May I help you?"

"I hope so. I am looking for a Mr. Kincaid, and I thought perhaps some court records may be able to help me find him."

"And your name, sir?"

"They call me Lance."

The judge did not ask for a last name. He was well aware that many people preferred not to share last names with others, particularly if they had had a brush with the law or were on the outs with the military occupation of the area.

"I take it you are not kin to Mr. Kincaid, since you don't seem to know his first name."

"Not that I know of," Lance replied, with some degree of honesty.

"We made a quick check of our records, and find no Kincaid in them. Of course, unless he applied for a marriage license, owns property, or pays taxes, he would not show up in our records."

"How far back do your records go?" Lance asked.

"Unfortunately, many of the records were destroyed in a fire just after the end of the war."

From the judge's reaction to his inquiry, Lance could see that he was not interested in providing any information, or worse, he was trying to hide something. He thanked the judge for his trouble, turned, and left the courthouse. He was sure that information about his father was known and for some reason it was being kept from him.

Hefty was in camp when Lance returned, and Lance could see that he couldn't wait to talk to him. "I sure got an earful at Payne's store. Bell County is under military law. At least, that's the official word, but in reality, it is being controlled by a scallywag named Hiram Christian."

"I think I've already had the pleasure of meeting Mr. Christian. He's a judge at the courthouse, but he was no help in finding any information about my pa." Lance said.

"I found out Bull Turner is on Christian's payroll, Hefty said. "The folks in the store say the federal soldiers carry out Christian's orders. They have levied excessive taxes on the landowners, and those that can't or won't pay are run off, and the property is handed out to Christian's favorites. If the land is choice enough, he keeps it for himself. Since there is no local or state elected government, the people have no recourse to what is going on."

"This sounds like your Regulators all over again, Hefty. Our best bet is to get to know some of the townspeople and see if we can get a lead on my father's ranch. If it's anywhere in the county, surely someone will know of it."

"I have a feeling that some of the locals may not be anxious to discuss it, for fear of the hired guns that Christian is using to enforce the law. We may be luckier in finding federal soldiers who are willing to do some talking" Hefty replied.

Lance nodded. "You may be right. Let's look around for some work; we're running a little low on cash. Besides, it will give us a chance to get to know some folks, and maybe rub shoulders with some of the federal troops."

That afternoon Lance and Hefty made their way to Payne's Mercantile. Hefty introduced Lance to Sam Payne, and asked if there was any work to be had around the county.

"I don't suppose you have any logging experience, do you?" Payne asked.

Lance and Hefty looked at each other and grinned. "That's the kind of work that paid the bills to get us here," Lance said.

"Well then, you can have all the work you can handle. Because of all the Waco–Austin travel, the county is building better roads and creek crossings. They are looking for men to provide the timbers from the local brakes, and they're paying a dollar twenty-five per day plus evening meals at the hotel."

"I think they have just found two more strong backs to do the timbering," Lance said.

"Go talk to Silas Baggett out at the bridge site on the Belton–Waco road. Tell him Sam Payne sent you. Be prepared to go to work," Payne said.

"Much obliged, Mr. Payne. We will be there come sunup tomorrow," Lance said.

"No need to thank me. I'll expect to get a part of your wages when you come in for supplies," he laughed.

Lance and Hefty turned and started for the door then Lance stopped and took a few steps back toward Mr. Payne and hesitated.

"Is there a problem?" Mr. Payne said.

Lance was trying to decide just how much of his business he should share with Payne. He thought it would do no harm to let him know he was looking for someone.

"Who are some of the old-timers that were here in Bell County before the war?" Lance asked.

Payne hesitated and looked inquisitively at Lance before saying, "Why do you ask?"

"I'm trying to find the whereabouts of a Mr. Kincaid."

"I haven't been here long, but the name is not familiar to me. Some of the old timers may be able to help you. Let's see, there's the Childers family, Judge Tayler, Colonel Aiken, and the Potts family, to name a few."

"The courthouse shows no record of such a person, Lance said.

"You mean the court records that exist show no Mr. Kincaid," replied Payne.

"I heard that some of the records were lost in a fire," Lance said cautiously.

Payne shook his head. "The fire is not the problem. Many of the records were destroyed and replaced with deeds that indicate the scallywags and Regulators as owners," he said.

"This could be a real problem. If these Regulators are anything like the hoodlums that I dealt with in the East, they play for keeps. They have a lot at stake, and with the occupied law on their side they will be hard to whip," Hefty said.

"I'm not trying to whip anybody. I'm just trying to find my father, but I'll whip whoever tries to stop me," Lance said.

"This Mr. Kincaid is your father?" Payne asked.

Even though Lance had a good feeling about Sam Payne, he was disappointed that he had revealed that information to him. Taking a deep breath, he went on to explain his situation, with his part in the war and his loss of memory.

"I'd appreciate it if you'd keep this to yourself for the time being," he added. "I'm not anxious to have folks know too much about me, especially that I fought for the Union."

Payne nodded. "I understand; I am a loyal Texan, but I was against the secession. Sam Houston stood in this very square and tried to convince the crowd that seceding would be a big mistake. He said it was a hopeless situation that would end up in a bloodbath. The people would not listen to him. As a matter of fact, they threatened his life for saying what he did. I try not to fault people who live by what they believe. There are good folks who fought on both sides of the war. But I'm afraid my beliefs are not shared by many in these parts. You are wise in not being identified with either side. Now, to find out about your father, I think your best source of information would be Judge Tayler in Salado, just south of here. He and his wife have the first marriage license filed in Bell County. They have been very active in the community, and know most of the families in the county. He is one to walk the river with. You can trust him, and if he can help you, I'm sure he will."

"I appreciate your help, Mr. Payne. I think Hefty and I will be doing a little sightseeing down south soon."

"Lance!" Payne called as Lance turned to leave.

"Yes sir?"

"Do be careful. There is a lot on the line for these scallywags, and they will not hesitate to resort to violence. There have been a lot of people falsely put in prison or run out of the county. They will stop at nothing to get what they want."

"Well, I guess that's one thing we have in common. I'll stop at nothing to keep what I think is rightfully mine, whatever that may be."

The next few days they cut trees and used Baggett's horse team to drag the timbers to the bridge site. They both did the best they could to mix with the workers and be good listeners. Most of the stories were the same. Young men had returned from the war; they had no jobs and had lost their property. They were working to feed their families. They felt helpless under the rule of the Reconstruction laws of Congress. Texas had become a part of the fifth military district, and General Phil Sheridan was in command at his headquarters in New Orleans. Four thousand troops had been dispatched to Texas under the immediate command of General Charles Griffin, whose headquarters were in Galveston. All those who had served in the Confederacy were removed from office and replaced with military appointees. A combination of ignorance, vengeance, lack of concern, and greed on the part of the federal appointed representatives was destroying the social and economic base of the state of Texas.

During his highway work, Lance found out little to help him find his father. He did learn, however, that a place known as Three Forks on the trail to Salado was the hiding place of a group of troublemakers. These men had returned from the war and decided that holdups and highway robberies were easy ways to make a living. They had holed up in groves of cedars and dense thickets of dogwood and haw, and were formidable enough to discourage law enforcement from going in after them. They were careful to target the locals, and stayed away from the federal property. That kept the army off their tails.

After two weeks working for Baggett, Lance decided it was time to look into Salado, and suggested they leave at sunup. He was sure there were still answers to be found at the courthouse, but he had to have more information to know what to look for.

Hefty agreed with Lance's plan, and told Lance that he was feeling a little uneasy in Belton. "I can't say I have that 'hair on the back of the neck' feeling that you get, but something is not right here. Ever since we had dinner at the hotel, I've a hunch that someone has been watching us."

"You're half right, Hefty. We're bein' watched, all right, but it's more than one person, and I'm not sure they're working together. They've shown up at different times and in different places. I've never seen them together and I haven't gotten a good look at either one of them

"I've never felt so popular," Hefty replied.

The next morning they headed southeast along Nolan Creek and soon reached the point where the Lampasas and the Salado came together to form the Little River.

"From what we've been told, I think we're at Three Forks, where that outlaw bunch call home," Lance said. "From here, we follow the Salado to reach the town. The locals may have their eye on us. Let's mind our own business. Maybe if we leave them alone, they'll leave us alone."

Lance and Hefty's timing couldn't have been better. A large number of the outlaws were on a raid at the town of Heidenheimer, to the east. Four men were left to look after their hideout. However, without warning, the four showed up on horseback on the road and approached Lance and Hefty.

As Lance and Hefty pulled up, Lance took in the four. They were a motley crew. From the looks and smell of them, they hadn't washed in a coon's age. They had rifles across their saddles that needed a lot of attention. All four were heavily bearded, with ample tobacco stains on their whiskers.

One of the men said curtly, "What's your business here?"

"It's just that—our business," Lance replied.

"That kind 'a smart mouth could get a fella kilt," their spokesman said.

Lance felt sure any sign of weakness was going to cost them their outfits if not their lives.

"If you boys are thinkin' of doing the killing, you're going to need some help," Lance said.

"Maybe you ain't done your numbers. There's four of us and only two of you."

Lance moved his left hand up and rubbed his chin. Hefty knew what was coming, and prepared himself. Lance drew his Colt so fast the four had no time to react.

With the revolver aimed at the breastbone of the man that was doing the talking, Lance said, "With this piece, I count it six to four. You best do a re-count."

The renegade shot a quick glance at the other three and saw that their rifles were still resting across their saddles.

"Well, since Daily ain't here to decide what to do with you, we'll let you pass this time," he said.

"Now that's mighty big of you boys," replied Lance easily. "It's not often a feller meets up with fine upstanding citizens such as you."

Lance held his ground until the four men separated to let him and Hefty through. As they passed by the men, Lance rolled his mare around and backed her to the bend in the road. The four men looked on, but made no move to their weapons.

After turning the bend, Hefty said, "I heard that name 'Daily' mentioned at the mercantile. Seems he's the ringleader of a bunch of outlaws that hang out in these cedar brakes. He must be out raising a ruckus somewhere else. Lucky for us."

"We'll stay shy of this area if we need to make our way back to Belton," Lance said, and Hefty agreed.

They rode on and didn't see any sign of their greeting party the rest of the day. By midday they came to several springs that fed into the bubbling Salado creek. As they approached the north bank of the creek, they could see the town on the south bank. There was a cable suspension footbridge for pedestrian crossing, but horsemen and wagons had to use the old military crossing through the shallow waters to reach the south bank. They crossed the swift-moving water just above the manmade dam,

and walked their horses down the main street toward Salado College. The streets were alive with
people going about their shopping and visiting at
the corner mercantile. The town looked to be made
up of industrious, honest, religious folks, and had
the reputation of being a community of high character.

They rode by several cabins made of hand-
hewn, square-cut cedar logs joined by wooden pegs.
Each cabin had a chimney made of native stone.
Farther down the street they passed the Stagecoach
Inn. Its frontier architecture included a galleried
porch with a second-story balustrade. Locals
boasted that earlier guests at the inn included Robert
E. Lee and George Armstrong Custer. Since the
Chisholm Trail passed nearby, the cattle baron
Shanghai Pierce had also been a guest of the inn.

Just beyond the hotel was a one-story stone
building with a shingle-covered front porch. Hanging from the porch support was a sign reading "O.
T. Tayler, County Judge." Lance and Hefty entered
the front door, and saw a distinguished-looking man
sitting before a large oak rolltop desk. He had gray
hair and a full gray beard. His eyes were blue and
kindly. He turned to the men and asked, "May I
help you gentlemen?"

"We're looking for Judge Tayler," Lance replied.

"I'm sorry; he is not in just now. Can I be of
some help?"

"Thank you, but I really need to talk to the

judge on a personal matter. Do you know where I can find him?"

"He may be at home. He lives just down the street on the right. It's the large two-story white home. I'm sure he would be glad to help you if he can."

Lance thanked the man, and they returned to their horses. Just down the street they came to the judge's home. It was made of wood siding, freshly painted white. A low stone wall and walkway led up to the front porch. There was no hitching rail, so Lance asked Hefty to stay with the horses.

As Lance ascended the steps and approached the front door, Hefty glanced back down the street to see a lone rider pull up in front of the judge's office. It was too far to get a good look at him, but he watched the man as he stopped to roll a smoke, looked down the street in Hefty's direction, and entered the office.

Lance's knock was answered by a well-dressed lady who appeared to be in her late fifties. She had the appearance of aristocracy and an air of confidence, and she held unwavering eye contact with Lance as she greeted him. Lance could not help but feel that he was being appraised as she asked his business.

"I would like a minute with the judge concerning a personal matter," Lance said.

She must have approved of what she saw, Lance thought.

"Won't you come in and make yourself comfortable? I'll tell the judge you're here. Who shall I say is calling?"

"A friend of Mr. Kincaid," Lance replied after a moment of hesitation.

Mrs. Tayler left the room, and shortly thereafter Judge Tayler walked in and introduced himself. He had thick gray hair, a full beard, carried himself erect, and appeared to be in his early sixties.

"My wife tells me you are a friend of a Mr. Kincaid, but I'm afraid I have not had the pleasure of meeting your Mr. Kincaid," the judge said, shaking Lance's hand. "What is your business with him?"

For some reason, Lance felt no need to hold back information. There was an air about the judge that told Lance he was a man of principle who could be trusted.

"Mr. Payne at the Belton mercantile suggested I come to see you. Mr. Kincaid is my father."

The judge kept a critical eye on Lance, as if to evaluate his sincerity. Lance explained his loss of memory and his desire to locate his father in an effort to bring back his past. The judge listened to Lance intently, and his eyes showed genuine concern for his predicament.

"I know most of the people in town and many in the outlying area, but I'm sorry to say that the name Kincaid does not sound familiar. If your father makes his home in Bell County, I venture a guess that he does not live in Belton or Salado. I would also think that he has not been in the area long. Have you tried the court records at Belton?"

"Yes sir, I did but it seems all the records I was interested in were burned in the courthouse fire."

The judge just smiled shook his head and said, "The records were not destroyed by fire, that is, unless those in charge deliberately burned them. I hope you didn't tell them the purpose of your search."

"No sir, I simply told them I had a message from Fort Griffin for a Mr. Kincaid, who was thought to live in Bell County."

"Good! The fewer people who know your situation, the safer it will be for you. The county is full of fraudulent and unethical activities as a result of this Reconstruction. There is no limit to what some will do for financial gain. I suspect those in charge of property and taxes in the county may be corrupt. If you learn of any foul play, I suggest you get help from the federal troops in Austin. I'm sorry I can't be of more help in locating your father, but I do have a suggestion. Dr. Barton has been the only physician in Salado for several years. There is a good chance, if your father is anywhere in the area and has been in need of medical assistance, he would have called on Dr. Barton."

Lance smiled ruefully. "At least I'm beginning to learn where my pa isn't. That's more than I knew when I got to this county."

"I must warn you, Mr. Kincaid—uh, Lance— this is taking on the look of scallywags' doings. To not have courthouse records is one thing, but to say they were burned hints of skullduggery."

"I've heard of some of the underhanded practices," Lance replied.

"You haven't heard the half of it. They have friends in high places, and they play for high stakes. I'm certain the federal government does not endorse their practices. Unfortunately, due to manpower shortages, the government had to look for support from the civilian population. Many of these appointed people either turn a deaf ear to the needs of the locals or play 'get even' with the Texans for supporting the Confederate cause. Your situation is made more difficult, since you don't even know which side your father stood for."

"I'm not even sure which side I believed in," Lance admitted. "I was in the Union army, and sure think every man has the right to be free, but I must have been a Texan also. My partner with our horses out front is a straightforward case. He was a Yankee from Pittsburgh and in the Union army with me. But I have yet to find myself."

"Your friend is in enemy territory. We haven't convinced many in Texas the war is over and we lost. You are both lucky to have a friend at your side. You may need each other to cover your back trail. Bushwhacking is not an uncommon event in these parts."

"It's interesting you say that. I have had the feeling that we are being followed, but I'm not sure by who, or why."

"My guess is someone is trying to find out your purpose for being in the county. If they think you

are getting too close to information they are protect-
ing, your life won't be worth much."

"I'm going to get that information; good or bad;
I'm going to get it. If it's bad news, their life won't
be worth much," Lance said grimly.

"The odds are against you, Lance, but for some
reason, I believe you."

"Thanks again for your help."

"Go with God, Mr. Kincaid, and do be careful."

"I'll do that."

As Lance walked toward Hefty and the horses,
he was thinking about what the judge had said concerning his odds. Lance was not a gambling man.
When he found himself in a game of chance, he was
always smart enough to keep the odds in his favor.
He felt no differently about it now. He would get to
the bottom of this situation, but he would always
make his move with the best odds he could muster.

As Lance was mounting up, Hefty told him
about the lone rider at the judge's office. "His horse
is tied up at . . . well, I'll swear, the horse is gone,"
Hefty said.

"Did you get a look at him?"

"Not a good one. He was too far away. Looked
like a man in his thirties; moved like a cat, about
your build."

"Unless I miss my guess, we'll be seeing more
of him," Lance said.

As they rode back up the street to the home of
Dr. Barton, Lance asked Hefty, as he had several
times before, if he was sure he wanted to stay

hitched up to Lance's quest. Hefty made light of his question and said he was a lot safer in this "Reb" country with Lance than he would be alone. Lance wasn't sure that was true, but he decided not to argue the issue.

They tied their horses to the rail and walked up to the door. The doctor's house was a two-story redbrick built several hundred feet off the main street. The path to his house was bordered on both sides by a well-groomed lawn and rows of brightly colored flowers. The first floor was his office, and the second floor his residence. It was conveniently located near the Salado College, where the doctor was a trustee.

Before knocking on the door Lance turned to Hefty with a warning. "There're a lot of things that aren't setting well with me just now. Things may be getting a little testy. Something tells me my pa may have met with foul play. We best keep a sharp eye out, especially for those dudes who are following us. If they are back shooters, let's not give them a back to shoot at."

"I hate it when you get those feelings."

Doctor Barton answered their knock with a warm smile and a kind word, asking what he could do for them.

"Doctor Barton, my name is Lance, and this is my partner, Hefty. Judge Tayler suggested that I ask you about a man that I have a message for. I was told he lives in Bell County, but so far I haven't been able to locate him. The judge didn't know him and he thought you might."

"What is the man's name?"

"I only know his last name. It's Kincaid."

"Kincaid, Kincaid. . . The name sounds familiar. Come in and take a load off while I check my records."

He led them into his office, a large room with several comfortable chairs for his patients and a large, dark-colored rolltop desk where he kept his records. The walls held a number of certificates declaring the doctor's qualifications. There were also photographs showing his ties to the community and the college. Two floor-to-ceiling windows let the sunlight stream into the room and gave it a bright and cheery feeling. Lance couldn't help but feel encouraged as the doctor thumbed through his patient records.

"Ah yes! Here it is. Luke Kincaid. I remember him now. It was about eighteen months ago. He came to me with a nasty cut on the back of his head that required sixteen stitches. I asked him how it happened. He said he was breaking one of his young horses and forgot to keep his mind in the middle, whatever that means."

"I know what that means, Doc," Lance smiled. "I was told all it takes to ride a horse is to keep your left leg on the left side, your right leg on the right side, and your mind in the middle."

"Do you remember who gave you that advice?" Hefty asked.

"No, but I'll bet it was Pa. Maybe there is hope

for that memory of mine after all."

"You're a little young to be having memory problems, son," Doctor Barton said, looking at him curiously.

"I'm a lot older than I look, Doc. Do you know where this Luke Kincaid lives?"

"Not exactly. He was a nice enough sort, but kinda private."

"Why does that not surprise me?" Hefty said.

"What do you mean by that?" the doc asked.

"Nothing at all, Doc, just a private joke."

"You must at least have some idea which direction he came from or went to," Lance pressed the doctor.

"He said he rode all the way from the north fork of the Salado Creek. Quite a sight when he got here. He had tied a bandana around his head and under his chin to hold the wound together and stop the bleeding. His shirt was covered with blood, and he was looking mighty pale. He was one tough hombre—didn't even flinch as I was doing the stitching. He was insisting on turning right around and going back to his ranch. He said something about expecting visitors that he didn't want to miss. I insisted he stay for dinner, and he accepted. That gave him an extra hour or so to get his bearings before he headed out."

"Have you seen him in town since then?" Lanced asked.

"No, sure haven't. I told him to come back in a couple weeks and have the stitches removed, but he thanked me and told me he could take care of that."

"Could you tell me how to get to the north fork?"

"Certainly, just go back uptown to the Salado and head west for about fifteen miles. The water coming in from the northwest is the north fork of Salado Creek. Good grazing land. A fella could do well with some cattle on that land."

Lance rose to leave. "Thank you, Doc. You've been a great help. Hefty and I will be heading out that way."

"You know, boys, you have burned the better part of the daylight today. There's no moon tonight. You would be better off getting a good meal at the inn and lighting out early in the morning."

"Say Lance, that sounds like good advice. Some fine store-bought groceries would taste mighty good about now," Hefty said.

"Doc, it sounds like you make a habit of seeing that your visitors and patients get off to a good start," Lance said, shaking the doc's hand.

"Just a suggestion." He showed them to the door, wishing them well.

Lance was anxious to get moving. He guessed he was close to some answers after all this searching, but he knew the doc was right. Without a moon, it would be difficult making any distance along Salado Creek. He took a deep breath, tried to control his druthers, and decided morning would be soon enough. Lance and Hefty backtracked up the street to the Stagecoach Inn.

After treating themselves to a hot bath at the inn, they enjoyed a fine home-cooked meal of beef, biscuits, gravy, fresh bread, and coffee that could float a horseshoe. While they were nursing their third cup, Lance mused, "I wonder what my father will think of Amy?"

"First things first, partner. You don't even know what your pa is going to think of you."

"Aw, I guess you're right," Lance admitted ruefully. As a matter of fact, he wasn't sure what he thought of himself. He sat there and turned over in his mind what he knew about himself. It wasn't much—the war, the Schroeder family, Wood's tavern, meeting up with Hefty, his time with Amy, Dark Moon's vision and his ever-recurring dream. It sure wasn't much to account for a man in his thirties. He hoped that seeing his pa would bring it all back.

They finished their meal and hit the trail. After traveling about five miles they picked a site near the river for a camp that gave them visibility in all directions, to reduce the possibility of any unwanted visitors. They unsaddled the horses and rubbed them down with dry grass, then picketed them near some good grazing and within reach of the river. Hefty boiled up some strong coffee, and they each picked a spot for their bedrolls.

As they were finishing their coffee, Hefty said, "I guess you've been doing a lot of praying to reach this point. Maybe tomorrow will be your lucky day."

Lance looked into his cup for a spell and replied, "I don't have much truck with praying. I figure if someone somewhere put us here, He did so with the intent of putting us in charge of ourselves. Most of the preachers that I knew in Illinois tried to make themselves needed by developing all these different interpretations of the Good Book. It seems to me if He wanted us to follow His book, He would've seen to it that we all could understand it. Back at Schroeder's farm I read about an old religious man who lived about twenty-five hundred years ago. His philosophy was pretty simple. Be kind, be generous, do no harm, and seek your own happiness. It works for me."

"There are a few men with holes in them that would say you didn't live up to your standards," Hefty objected.

"I value my well-being. I will always take whatever steps necessary to protect myself and those around me who become victims of unjust treatment," Lance said ardently, then laughed at himself. "I'll swear, Hefty, I've been hanging around you so much, I'm starting to talk as much as you do."

"That'll be the day," Hefty said, as he added a little more wood to the fire and headed for his bedroll.

Lance lay there, staring up at the sky, unable to sleep. His mind was swirling with thoughts of what might lie ahead of him. He realized just how long he had been awake when he noticed the fire had died down enough to make the stars shine like diamonds on black velvet.

"I wonder if Amy is looking at the same stars about now," he said to himself as he drifted off to sleep.

CHAPTER 15

Several hours before dawn, Lance woke up without stirring, as he was prone to do. He lay motionless for several minutes, listening for any sounds that shouldn't be there. Satisfied with the silence, he rolled out from under his blanket, stood up, and was shocked to full consciousness by what he saw. In the moonlight he could see the highline Hefty had tied for the horses, but the horses were gone.

"Hefty! Wake up. We got us a problem."

Hefty sprang from his bedroll, rifle in hand.

"What's going on?"

"It looks like we're afoot," Lance groaned.

"Dag nab it! I had a feeling about the horses when I turned in. Look here, I tied a lead from Toni to my wrist. It's still on my wrist. Someone cut it near the halter and tied it to the highline."

"It'll be 'can see' soon. There's not much we can do 'til then. Let's get some breakfast and check for tracks at first light," Lance said.

They were careful not to disturb the area around the highline so they could read any sign left by the horse thieves. Soon a soft gray light began to move across the treetops, and there was enough light to make out tracks. Lance searched the ground near the horses.

"We may be in luck," he said as he knelt down to study the footprints in the sandy soil.

"We sure could use some," Hefty replied.

"There's only one set of moccasin tracks."

"How does that make us lucky?"

"An Indian traveling alone is unusual. Most likely this was a case of a lone Indian being shamed by the band for not counting coup on one of their raids. He has left the band to try and redeem himself. By returning with these horses he can regain the respect of the other warriors."

"I still don't see how that makes us lucky."

Lance sat back on his haunches. "There's a good chance he'll not expect us to follow him, since we're foot. He may also be taking the horses back to his band, which could be nearby."

"So we catch up with the band. How do you propose we get our mounts back?"

"We'll worry about that when we catch up with them."

After stashing their saddles and gear, they

headed out, following the tracks of their two horses. The sign was easy to follow, since it was tracks of one shod horse and one barefoot. They traveled light, with only water, revolvers, and enough rope to fashion a couple of bridles. It was close to sundown when they smelled smoke.

"This may be payday. From here on in, keep your eyes and ears open. If they're holed up here, they'll probably have some lookouts on the edge of their camp," Lance whispered.

Moving on their bellies, they topped a brush-covered rise. The band of ten or twelve was camped near a small stream. As they approached from the south, they could see horses tied to a highline about fifty yards to the east. Bess and Toni were among the horses, and one Indian was sitting near the animals to keep them secure.

"There's only one brave guarding the horses. We should be able to take him out," Hefty whispered.

"We might be able to, but if we alert the others we'll be in deep trouble. Besides, we need to handle that lookout before we tackle the one guarding the horses," Lance replied.

"What lookout?"

"Look about a hundred yards at three o'clock in those trees."

"Well, I'll swear! You have better eyes than I do."

Both men studied the lay of the land in silence for a minute or two, and then Hefty got a big grin on his face.

"I've got an idea," he said.

"Let's hear it."

"That lookout you spotted has a bow with him. If we could injun up on him and get the bow, I believe I could drop the horse guard. It's about a fifty-yard shot across that clearing. There's a good chance, with night fall coming on, we could get in and out without being detected."

"Are you that good with a bow?"

"I guess now would be a good time for you to find out."

"It looks like our best chance. Let's go for it," Lance said. "Lay low while I work my way around that lookout. I'll come on him from the backside. Once I best him, I'll signal you to move up for that shot at the horse guard," Lance said, taking his skinning knife from its sheath.

"I thought you said you didn't hold with knifings," Hefty said.

"I said I didn't like it; I didn't say I wouldn't do it if necessary and it still may not be necessary."

With that comment, Lance disappeared into the brush. He inspected each area of his footfalls to make sure no sound would be made. Thirty feet from the brave, Lance began to belly up from behind. The lookout was distracted enough by his camp activity to give Lance an edge.

Lance stood up with his knife in a throwing position and approached the Indian. Now he was close enough to bring the handle of his knife down full force on the back of the man's head. The lookout collapsed to the ground without a sound. Lance waved Hefty in. They gathered up the lookout's bow and the quiver of arrows. After moving out of sight of the horse guard, Hefty said, "I'm going to release one arrow to get a feel for the bow's tension. I'll put the next arrow in our target."

Hefty let fly an arrow at a tree that was just about the distance between him and the guard. The arrow was on line and just below the fork in the tree at which he had aimed.

"This bow will do just fine," he said.

The evening light was fast fading as Hefty moved into position for his shot. The shadows were long and visibility was poor. Selecting the truest arrow in the quiver, he waited for a broadside view of the target. After notching the arrow to the string, he raised the bow overhead and began to lower it, drawing back the string. When the arrow was aligned with the target, he released the arrow.

Whissh!

The guard turned about forty-five degrees and fell face down without a sound. The arrow had entered his back just under the left shoulder blade and penetrated deep into his body.

Lance and Hefty could hear the voices of the other men around the campfire as they reached their horses. Seconds later they were leading their mounts away from the camp. As soon as they reached a safe distance, they grabbed some mane, swung up on the horses' backs, and headed back to their stash at a brisk gallop, using their rope-made bridles for control.

"We need to pack up and move out as soon as possible. There's no tellin' how long it will take before our actions are discovered," Lance said.

They were on the trail searching for the ranch and out of harms way before daylight.

"I'm sure glad that wasn't just a story about you being handy with a bow," Lance remarked as they slowed up, the late morning sun warming their backs.

"I have to admit, with the light being what it was, that was one of my testiest shots."

"Well, you certainly passed the test."

With the sun high in the sky and a good twelve hours behind them, Lance decided the horses needed a wind break. They stopped long enough to boil up some coffee and eat some jerky. Lance looked over the countryside as he finished his coffee. The morning was crisp with a light breeze out of the north. The air smelled of rain but there was not a cloud in site. A tall stand of prairie grass covered the rolling hills for as far as he could see. It certainly looked like prime cattle country. Later that morning, while riding along the Salado River, Lance pulled up.

"What do you see, Lance?"

"It's not what I see, it's what I smell."

Lance swung out of the saddle and began to examine the damp green growth along the river. He bent over and pulled up some small green leaves and took a whiff of them.

"Mint! This is mint," Lance said.

"Yep, sure is. I smelled it myself a ways back. So what?"

"The doctors told me it wasn't likely I would get all my recall back quick like. They told me I would probably remember smells or sounds before I recognized familiar sights. I think this is one of those smells. Wherever I lived, there was a lot of mint. I'm sure of it."

"Well, that's a start."

Lance's pulse raced and his face flushed as he breathed in his first hint of his past. He tried in vain to bring up any visions.

"I know we're close, Hefty. I can feel it. Let's leave the creek bank and ride northwest for a while."

"Lead the way, partner."

As they rode, they came upon a herd of long-horn cattle that carried a rocking R brand.

$$\underline{R}$$

Lance decided to backtrack them and try to find the ranch headquarters. He hoped those folks could direct him to his father's ranch.

"If your pa has a spread near here, he picked a good spot. Plenty of good grazing with nice stands of live oak for shade. And plenty of water, with the Salado close by."

Lance barely heard Hefty's comments. He was preoccupied with the brand on the cattle. He wasn't sure what is was, but something bothered him about that brand.

As they came over a swell, they spotted a ranch house with several outbuildings about a mile off. They picked the horses up to a trot, and headed for what looked like the ranch headquarters. About a hundred yards from the buildings they came to a fence and gate entry. Above the entry was an arch with a large reproduction of the rocking R brand in the center. Lance stopped at the entry and studied the brand for a minute, then moved on toward the ranch house. After passing a creaking windmill and large stock tank, they approached the buildings. Lance noticed the structures and the fences were in need of repair. Apparently the owners took no pride in their outfit.

"Hello the ranch house!" Lance called, as they came up to the hitching rail.

A few seconds later, a tall rangy cowboy stepped out onto the porch. He was wearing a tied-down hog leg that dwarfed his frame. His narrow shoulders and close-set eyes gave him the appearance of a snake. Without a hint of welcome, he fixed his eyes on Lance and said, "This here is private property. Unless you have business here, I'll thank you to move on."

Lance could see that Hefty did not take kindly to the abrupt attitude of the cowboy, and was about to let him know it. Before Hefty could get a word out, Lance calmly explained that they were looking to get a message to a rancher in the area by the name of Luke Kincaid. He saw the cowboy tense when he heard the name. After a short hesitation, he replied, "And just who are you? As he spoke his hand slowly moved closer to his revolver and he took a wider stance.

"Just someone from Fort Griffin with a message for Mr. Kincaid."

"Well, you must be off course. I know this country and the people in it. There's no Kincaid in these parts."

From his hesitation and his defensive posture, Lance had no doubt the cowboy was lying, but he decided there would be little to gain by forcing the issue.

"Guess we were given some bad directions. Sorry to bother you," Lance said.

Hefty was about to make a comment when he caught a look from Lance that told him to hold up.

"If I were you, I'd be a mite careful about coming up on the ranches around here without an invite," the rancher added with an unpleasant smile. "It could be bad for your health."

"Thanks for the advice. I'll surely give it some consideration in the future," Lance replied.

Hefty followed Lance's lead, turned his horse, and rode out the way they came in. As they reached the gate, he said, "That ol' boy was lying through his teeth. Couldn't you see that?"

"I saw it," Lance replied grimly. "I also saw the man was no rancher. He wore his gun low and tied down. The front of his holster was cut out, and the leather was well oiled to allow a fast draw. Pushing him wouldn't have bought us anything but trouble.

That trouble may come, but I'll pick the time and place. I have a feeling I'm not finished dealing with that one."

As they rode off, Lance saw a lone rider come off the rise to the south, approach the ranch house, and enter the front door. "One of those tailing us is tied in with that gunman. He just joined him at the ranch," he said.

"I didn't see anybody," Hefty replied.

"Trust me. And he is not the man you saw in Salado. That man was a size and a half of me," Lance said.

After riding on for about a half mile, Lance turned, looked over his back trail, and said, "I can't explain it, but I get a feeling this is a special place in my past. I smelled that mint, then that feeling got reinforced when I heard that windmill squeak."

"A lot of windmills squeak."

"Not like that one. It was the wooden rig that was squeaking, not the metal parts. I don't think we need to look any further; we just need to dig deeper."

"What do you have in mind?"

"First we need to lose whoever is tailing us. Then we will double back, stay to the low country, and check out this ranch."

"I ain't too busy," Hefty said, waiting for Lance to take the lead.

They returned to the Salado, traveled upstream some distance to a gravel bank, and exited the river on the far side. After traveling a few hundred yards, they rode onto a rocky area that left few tracks. Before leaving the rocky area they turned back toward the river, taking a different route. As they started back, Lance led Hefty's horse as Hefty walked behind them, brushing out any sign of tracks with some branches from a nearby hackberry tree. Then they reentered the creek and headed west, leaving the water once they reached a hard surface. Before leaving the hard ground, Lance dismounted, took several gunnysacks from his saddlebags, and tied them over his horse's hooves.

"So that's why you kept those grub sacks. You had this in mind all along," Hefty said.

"I thought they might come in handy. Since your horse has no shoes, when they do find our tracks, they won't see tracks of shod horses, and won't be sure they aren't a couple of Indian ponies."

They spent the next hour checking out the countryside, keeping below the skyline to avoid detection. They traveled through rolling hills covered with good grazing. Many of the draws had stands of tall hackberry and live oak trees. Several had running water from springs that fed into the Salado. They also came across several hundred head of Rocking R cattle. Hefty noticed that Lance seemed to be moving as though he had a destination in mind.

"Are you headed for somewhere special?" he finally asked.

"I'm not sure. I just have a feeling I need to be moving this way."

"I've sure learned to pay attention to your feelings," Hefty said.

By this time, they were five or six miles from the ranch house. Lance pulled up and looked ahead at a large live oak standing alone on top of a rise. It had a perfect shape, as though an artist had painted it. From that tree, he thought, you would be able see miles in all directions.

Without saying a word, Lance headed for the tree. Except for cattle, there was no evidence of traffic in the area for some time. As they crested the hill, Lance pulled up short spotting what looked like a grave marker in the shade of the tree. He stepped down and handed his reins to Hefty. His heart sank and he was flooded with despair as he approached close enough to read the inscription:

Here Lies
Luke Kincaid
Back Shot 1866

Lance stood silent and stared at the marker. His body shuddered, but he held back the tears as his mind shifted from denial, to acceptance, to sorrow, and finally to anger. Try as he might, he could not bring back the memory of his past or his father.

Hefty moved alongside Lance and said, "Sorry it had to end this way."

Lance continued to look at the marker without

saying a word. After several minutes, he said through clenched teeth, "This hasn't ended by a damn sight."

"I guess I should have figured that. Where do we go from here?" Hefty asked.

"This isn't your fight. There is no need for you to get involved. I appreciate all you've done, but I can't ask you to get mixed up in my private war."

"No need to ask me. I'm in for the long haul. Besides, I don't have anything to do anyway."

Lance let out a deep breath. "I gotta say, I'm glad you feel that way. I just may need someone to cover my back before this party is over."

"Like I said, where do we go from here?"

Lance seemed not to hear Hefty as he stood and looked at the marker, pondering the situation. Who shot his father, and why? And stranger yet, who went to the trouble of getting him a headstone and burying him? It surely wasn't the back shooter.

As Lance considered his next steps, he couldn't help but think about Dark Moon's prediction that his father would not be in his future. Finally he pulled Hefty's rifle from its scabbard, handed it to him, and said, "Think you can drop that heifer in the draw below us?"

"It's a fair distance, but I think this piece will handle it. We have plenty of grub. Why do you want to kill someone else's stock?"

"Just do it. I'll explain later."

Hefty shrugged, adjusted the sight for the distance, took careful aim at the animal, and squeezed off a round. The heifer fell like it was hit between the eyes with a twelve-pound Pittsburgh coal miner's sledgehammer. Without a word, Lance mounted up and moved off at a gallop toward the fallen animal. Hefty followed close behind. When they reached the cow, Lance dismounted, drew his knife, and began cutting away the hide on the left hip where the brand was located. As he peeled the hide back, he looked at the underside behind the brand.

"Just as I thought," Lance said. "Look at this."

"What am I suppose to be seeing, besides the wrong side of a cow?"

"Someone is mighty handy with a running iron. They altered the original brand. The original brand was the bar K

K

as in Luke Kincaid. It's been changed to the rocking R.

R

Father was probably murdered because he wouldn't let the shyster politicians take his ranch."

"All we need to do is find out who owns the Rocking R brand," Hefty said.

"It may not be that simple, but it's a good start." Lance stood. "I'm headed back to the Bell County Courthouse to check on that ownership. The Union troops in charge of the Confederate restoration are located in Austin. I doubt if they are a part of this land corruption. I'd like you to go to Austin and look up whoever is in charge. Tell them what we've found here, and see if they can send up the personnel necessary to straighten this mess out."

As Hefty checked his cinch and gathered up his reins he looked over his shoulder and said, "Sure I can do that, but won't you need me with you in Belton?"

"You'll be more help if you can bring up some federal muscle."

"Whatever you say. Don't go startin' the dance before I get back."

Lance was in the saddle and headed out at a gallop when he hollered back, "I'm not planning on it. I'm just going to do some quiet searching for more information."

As Hefty rode off, Lance headed back to his father's gravesite. He stepped down off Bess and stood next to his father's headstone trying in vain to bring back something from his past. He realized he was able to bring back familiar smells and sounds, but little else. He felt his intuition had led him to his father's grave, but he could not get his mind around any facts.

As he stood deep in thought, he became aware of a lone rider on the ridge to the north. It was not the same rider he had seen enter the ranch house as they left the Rocking R ranch. He did not believe the rider had tracked them to the site. It was almost as though he knew of the grave and was there waiting to see if Lance would find it.

Watching the other man, he thought, "One of these days soon, I'm going to meet up with that rider, and maybe then I will have some questions answered." Lanced gathered up his reins, mounted up, and headed back for Belton.

CHAPTER 16

Hefty was surprised at the large number of federal troops as he entered Austin. The headquarters for the Reconstruction was in Galveston under General J. J. Reynolds. Reynolds had some four thousand troops under his command to assist him in enforcing the infamous "Reconstruction Laws of Congress." The Southern states had initially been divided into five districts and placed under the control of the military. General Phil Sheridan was in charge of District Five, made up of Louisiana and Texas, with the headquarters in New Orleans. Sheridan and his self-appointed civil-government representatives had full civil and military power over the district. Reynolds was Sheridan's replacement, and some said he was more set on punishing the Confederacy then on reconstructing it.

Hefty decided to "test the water" by taking a place at the bar of the Pink Garter Saloon and sharing a drink or two with the locals. He soon discovered it was not going to be an easy task to find support for correcting some Northern injustice to a Texas rancher. He did have the advantage of having been a Union soldier. That enabled him to be accepted by his pro-Union companions at the saloon. After some discussion, he was able to determine whom he shouldn't talk to, and he even heard some names dropped of individuals who were more sympathetic toward the Southern cause. One of these was an officer who was a born and reared Texan who had fought on the side of the Union because he didn't believe in slavery. It seemed to Hefty that would be a good place to start. The name was Colonel Angus Chandler.

Hefty finished his drink and left the soldiers at the bar that were solving the world's problems. He was surprised to find such lack of dedication to the job they were assigned to do. It was obvious that the temptation of land grabbing and payoffs was too appealing to the visiting Yankees. He was sure there must be some who were focused on true reconstruction. He hoped that Colonel Chandler would be one. As he rode toward the military headquarters, he rehearsed in his mind the message he wanted to get across to the colonel.

The private at the gate directed him to Colonel Chandler's office. The buildings being used as the headquarters were originally built by the city, and had previously housed the local government officials. But all duly elected positions were eliminated by the Reconstruction teams and replaced with officials named by General Sheridan. The general had made a point of selecting those with little or no sympathies for the South.

Hefty entered the two-story stone building and followed the signs to Colonel Chandler's office. A sergeant sitting behind an oak desk occupied the front office.

"What can I do for you?" the sergeant asked.

"I would like to speak to the colonel about some ranch property that may have been fraudulently obtained up north in Bell County."

"Just fill out this claim and I will have the colonel take it under consideration."

Hefty knew that would be a dead end. That claim would end up in a file, to eventually be thrown away before anybody looked at it. Returning the paper to the man, he said firmly, "Sergeant, one man has been murdered, and another man's life is in danger over this swindle. It's important that I get a chance to present this information to Colonel Chandler. If the federal authorities don't address this situation, it will likely turn into all-out war." He knew that was a stretch of the truth, but he was used to that in most of the stories he told.

The sergeant hesitated. A range war would be the kind of thing that could get back to President Johnson, and that could spell trouble for all those holding office on the Reconstruction team. He looked Hefty over, and asked his name, then said, "I'll see if the colonel will see you. Have a seat."

The sergeant entered the colonel's office and closed the door. A few minutes later he returned and said, "The colonel will see you." He motioned for Hefty to enter the office.

Hefty was immediately taken by the air of authority that the office and the colonel presented. The colonel stood up as Hefty approached his desk. He was a man well over six feet tall, and seemed taller from the way he carried himself. He appeared to be in his forties, with broad shoulders, a ruddy complexion, thinning blonde hair mixed in with some premature gray and clean shaven, with a hawkish look much like Andrew Jackson. He wore a well-kept full uniform with his hat and saber hanging on a hook just behind his chair. There was a revolver and a Bible on his desk among his stacks of papers. The office was a good size with a couch and several chairs. The walls were finished with fine wood paneling. One was covered with diplomas, certificates, and commendations. Nothing in the office was of a personal nature—no family pictures, and no indications of hobbies. This man seemed to be all business.

"What can I do for you, Mr. Forrest?"

"I'm here to seek the assistance of the federal government concerning the murder of a Bell County rancher and the confiscation of his ranch."

"Do you see this stack of papers on my desk?" the colonel responded bluntly.

Hefty nodded that he did.

"Most of these relate to cases of land and property illegally obtained. Most of them involve actions taken by the government-appointed Reconstructionists. I can only ask that you write up the details of your situation and submit them to my sergeant, and I will include them in my stack. I must admit, most of them do not involve murder. Was it kin of yours who was murdered?"

"Actually, Colonel, I am here to help out my partner. He is on his way to the Bell County Courthouse to check on the record of the current owner of his father's ranch. It was his father that was bushwhacked."

"Does your partner have a name?"

"Yes sir, it's Kincaid, Lance Kincaid."

The colonel started. "Any kin to Luke Kincaid?"

"Yes sir, Luke Kincaid was his father. He was the one who was back shot."

The colonel was speechless for a spell, looking down at his desk with deep concern. He slowly raised his head, a look of disbelief in his eyes as he said, "Luke and I rode for the Texas Rangers together. After all we survived, I never thought his life would end that way. I couldn't count how many times he saved my hide, either from the Comanches or some renegade cowboys. They would have had to shoot him in the back. I never saw the man good enough to best him face on."

"Sounds like Lance is a chip off the old block," Hefty replied.

The colonel called to his sergeant and asked not to be disturbed. He turned to Hefty and asked him for the details concerning this miscarriage of justice. Hefty filled him in on all that had taken place since arriving in Bell County. He told the colonel Lance was going to revisit the county seat to find out who was listed as the owner of his father's ranch.

The colonel grimaced. "I know enough about the problems in Bell County to assure you that your friend will get little satisfaction at the courthouse. As a matter of fact, I wouldn't be surprised if he doesn't already need our help."

"Then you will help, Colonel?"

"I intend to personally get to the bottom of this. I can only make recommendations concerning the murder. The arrests must be handled by the civil authorities. But I can take action on any illegal activity that may have occurred concerning the confiscation of land under the guise of Reconstruction. That's the least I can do for Luke. I can't believe he's gone.---- Meet me at the livery stable at sun up and we will head for Belton."

"Yes sir, I'll be there and ready to ride," Hefty replied.

CHAPTER 17

It was three days before Lance arrived back in Belton. He decided to stop first in Salado to pay another visit to Judge Tayler and fill him in on what he had discovered.

"I'm not surprised. It's no less than I expected," the judge said.

"I sent Hefty, my partner, to get help from the federal authorities."

"You've done the right thing in trying to get federal support, but I would discourage you from going to Belton alone. I suspect that the legal authorities in Belton are probably in on the scheme, and will provide you with little support."

"I appreciate your advice judge, but I feel I must get to the bottom of this before more evidence is altered or destroyed."

"You must do what you think is right, Mr. Kincaid. I only suggest you move ahead carefully."

"I intend to do that judge. Thanks again for all your help."

As Lance turned to leave the judge said, "Hope my help will make a difference."

"I'm sure it will. I hope the next time we meet it will be under more favorable circumstance."

With that, Lance left for Belton.

When he reached Belton, Lance entered the courthouse to find Judge Christian at the front desk going over some papers.

"Good morning, Judge."

Christian did not seem surprised to see him. As a matter of fact, it almost looked as though he was expecting Lance. He had an uneasy smile and began tapping his pencil on the desk.

"Good morning, uhhh, Lance, is it? Nice to see you again. How can I help you?"

Lance walked up to the desk looked down at Christian and exchanged no cordial greeting. His demeanor made it clear this was not to be a social visit.

"I would like to know who is on record as owner of the Rocking R Ranch."

"Certainly; that should be a matter of record. Just have a seat. I'll check our files and be right back."

It seemed to take more time than it should have, and Lance thought he heard a rear door close as he waited. After about five minutes, the judge returned, papers in hand. One of those papers looked to be a deed.

"Our records show the ranch to be owned by a Mr. Slade Cannon."

"Does it show who he bought the ranch from?"

"It appears that Mr. Cannon is the original owner. He acquired the land from the government."

"What is the date of that deed?"

"Let's see . . . oh yes, here it is: May 13, 1862."

"May I see that deed?"

"Certainly. Here you are."

Lance looked the deed over. It had the appearance of a legal transaction. But as he read down the property description, he noticed that at the bottom of the page, there was a line for the signature of the seller just above one for the buyer. That line looked to have been tampered with, and some entry had been erased.

"The seller line has no signature," Lance said.

"That's a standard form used for all purchases. In the case of land purchased from the government, no signature is necessary."

Just as Lance was going to question the judge further, the front door opened and two men walked in, followed by Bull Turner, the man that approached him and Hefty in the Saloon that first night in Belton. There was something different about Turner—he was wearing a badge.

"Lance, you're under arrest. I'll thank you for your gun," Turner said.

"What's the charge?" asked Lance, feeling his

stomach tighten.

"Cattle rustling! Now hand over that gun."

"That's ridiculous. If I'm a cattle rustler, where are the cattle?"

"We found one of them lying dead out on the range, half skinned, and a witness saw you at the heifer."

"Did they also see that the brand on that cow had been altered?"

"You'll get a chance to tell your story at your trial, if you live long enough to get one," he smirked. "Cattle rustlers are not tolerated in these parts. Now do you come along peaceful-like, or do I have to have my deputies drag you in?"

Without a word, Lance handed over his gun and walked toward the door, followed by the deputies and the sheriff. Somebody had gone out the back door of the courthouse to get Turner, and the trumped-up charge was leveled to get him out of the way until they could get more information on him, or maybe, better yet, get rid of him.

He had a feeling they had no intention of letting him reach a trial. There was little he could do now. He only hoped that Hefty would be coming soon with some federal support to sort this mess out.

CHAPTER 18

Colonel Chandler turned his duties over to his second in command, Major Stewart, and prepared to leave with Hefty and seven enlisted men, whom he personally selected. These were men the colonel knew to be soldiers dedicated to the true Reconstruction of the South. They headed out just after daybreak the next morning at a good pace that would get them to Belton in a little over two days, barring any trouble.

The colonel rode alongside Hefty and said, "Luke and I traveled this route many times in search of renegade Comanches and Apaches who occasionally raided this far east. Most of that kind of trouble is further west and north these days."

"Yes sir, we got to sample a little of that just north of Fort Griffin. Apparently, Lance was a

Texas Ranger just like his father. That saved our bacon when we found out that one of the raiding Apaches was an Indian that Lance had befriended before the war."

Chandler smiled. "Lance must take after his father. Luke had as many Indian friends as he had white friends. The Indians blamed the government for their problems, but somehow they never blamed Luke. Luke never harmed an Indian, or anybody else, for that matter, unless it couldn't be avoided."

"Well, somebody is going to be harmed in the fracas we are headed for, and I just hope it's not Lance," Hefty said.

"The sooner we get there, the better chance we have of preventing that, Mr. Forrest."

"Please just call me Hefty, Colonel."

"As you wish—Hefty. Forward at trot, men, we're burning daylight."

That evening, things were heating up in Belton. From inside the jail, Lance heard a ruckus growing in the town square, and he was able to stand on his bunk and see out through the tiny window. What he saw certainly got his attention. Slade Cannon had showed up on the square, and Lance recognized him as none other than the gunman who had confronted him and Hefty on the porch of the Rocking R Ranch. Cannon began to gather a crowd, claiming that "the man in the jail" had been rustling cattle on his ranch. The county had had their fill of renegades from Three Forks who were rustling their livestock. With patience wearing thin and tempers running high, the crowd was well on its way to taking the law into its own hands.

"I hope Hefty doesn't let the door hit him in the butt getting back here. He better have some legal muscle with him when he arrives," Lance said to himself, the knot in his stomach twisting.

The crowd became more vocal and began to talk of a hanging to save the judge the trouble. At Slade's urging, they began to move toward the jail. At least for the time being, Lance's fate was out of his hands. The sheriff was nowhere to be found, and Lance figured he certainly couldn't count on him to intervene anyway. But just as the crowd reached the front of the jailhouse, the owner of the mercantile, Sam Payne, stepped in front of them with a double-barrel scattergun cocked and pointed at the crowd. In particular it was pointed at Slade.

"Mr. Cannon, it seems to me you have got the folks a little riled and thinking wrong-headed," Payne said.

"You best keep to your store tending. This is none of your business. It wasn't your cattle that were rustled. And if I were you, I'd be a little careful who you point that scattergun at," Cannon replied.

"You cool down this crowd and I won't need to point it at all."

"What's your stake in this affair? Maybe you're in cahoots with that rustler inside."

That comment did not sit well with the crowd, however, since Payne was a well-known and respected citizen of Belton. He spoke to the crowd, but kept his eyes on Cannon.

"Folks, you know me, and you know I have no tolerance for the no-accounts that are hold up at Three Forks raising the devil with the local ranchers. I met the man you have in jail several weeks ago, and I believe he came here with no criminal intent. But if he is guilty of some crime, then the law should take due course. Don't take the law into your own hands. Judge Tayler is due here tomorrow. He will see that the man gets a fair hearing and trial if it's deemed necessary."

"We don't need to wait for Judge Tayler. Judge Christian is right here in town, and he would be glad to hold the hearing," replied Cannon from the crowd.

"Judge Christian is a municipal judge whose term has expired and is not authorized to address a criminal case." When Cannon did not back down, he added, "Well, what will it be, boys? Do we wait for the judge, or will I need to begin the party with this scattergun?"

After some grumbling and shouting, one of the townsfolk said, "I guess if he is guilty, he can just as well hang by the law as by us. I say we wait for the judge. It's not worth getting us after each other."

It was obvious Cannon was not happy with the reaction of the crowd. He tried to get the ear of a few of the crowd, but the edge was off, and they had resigned themselves to waiting it out. As the crowd disbanded, Cannon made his way to the courthouse and entered by a side door. Payne entered the jail and checked to see that Lance was safe and sound. He walked up to the cell door uncocking his shotgun keeping it out of reach of Lance.

"Mr. Payne, I owe you one. If it wasn't for you, I'd be hanging by one of those live oaks about now."

"This was not a personal thing, Lance. I would have done the same for any man. I just believe that times are changing, and the days of vigilante justice are in the past, or should be. If the courts find you guilty, I'll be the first to see that justice is carried out. But I pride myself on being a pretty good judge of character, and I don't believe you're a cattle rustler."

"You got that right, sir, but the less you know about this situation the safer you will be. It will all come out in the hearing."

"I'm concerned about you getting a fair hearing, Lance."

"I don't have all my eggs in that basket. Hefty should be on his way right now with some federal representation."

"I hope for your sake it is the right federal representation." He turned to leave. I" need to get back to my family. If Judge Tayler gets here in the morning, I'll feel better about this matter when I know he has a hand in it. In the meantime, try to protect your back, and don't put too much faith in Sheriff Turner, if he ever shows up. And there is something not right about this Slade Cannon. He was in town several days ago with a couple of seedy characters. They came by my store for some supplies, and I heard one of the men call him 'Daily'."

"Daily! That figures. He is 'El Jefe' of the Three Forks Gang. His men said as much when they tried to waylay Hefty and me on our way to Salado."

"That's even more reason for you to be careful. I do need to be getting back," Payne said.

He left the jailhouse and stepped out on the sidewalk, paused for a minute, and looked both directions along the street. Seeing no signs of trouble, he headed for his home just a few doors off the town square.

Lance paced the tiny cell, frustrated and restless. Finally, he told himself there was nothing he could do until the hearing. He would try to get some sleep. Little did he know how much he would need that sleep before this affair was over.

He stretched out on the bunk and put his hat over his face to shield the light of the full moon that was streaming through the cell window. He lay there turning over in his mind the events of the last few days. He knew his father had been killed by someone involved in stealing his ranch, and he was sure that Christian had something to do with it. There was no question in his mind that Sheriff Turner was being used to give the activity some legitimacy. He had two goals in his life right now—he must find his father's killer and get his father's ranch back.

Lance had just slipped off to a restless sleep

when he heard the front door to the jailhouse open. A moment later, the sheriff appeared in front of his cell.

"Kincaid, I don't know how long I'll be able to keep the town folks in control. It's my job to see that you are kept safe until the hearing and trial. I think you're an honest man, and I don't think for a minute that you rustled those cattle. If you'll give me your word that you will show up for the hearing in the morning, I'll release you."

There was something about the man's smile that Lance didn't like, but he said, "Well, Sheriff, I sure appreciate your confidence in me. I fully intend to be here for the hearing in the morning. I'd like to be here alive and kicking."

"I thought you'd feel that way, so I'll tell you what I'll do. It's too risky to have you leave by the front door. There are too many people out there just waiting to get their hands on you. My horse is out back, saddled and tied to the hitching post. You'll be able to ride him up the back street to the river, and then follow the river to the tall stand of hack-berries. From there you can head north out of site of the town folk and hide out until the hearing."

"I don't know how to thank you, Sheriff."

"It's the least I can do for you, Kincaid. I'll just come north and get you when the hearing time is set."

Turner took the cell keys from his hip and unlocked the cell. As Lance moved slowly out of the cell, his mind racing, Turner followed him to the back door. When they reached the door, the sheriff stepped in front of Lance and unlocked it with a second key from his key ring. He opened the door and pointed to the horse that was tied at the rail.

Lance was still in the dark of the doorway, but the full moon showered the area behind the jail with light. As he rubbed his chin with his left hand, he studied the situation before him. He took a step toward the door. Just as he came alongside the sheriff, he quickly relieved him of his six-shooter, stepped back, and pushed Turner through the door. A shot rang out as the sheriff stumbled out into the moonlight.

"Don't shoot, it's Turner," the sheriff shouted frantically.

Lance grabbed the sheriff around the neck, pulled him back into the hall, threw him to the floor, and slammed the door closed. Turner jumped to his feet and started toward Lance, until he found himself looking down the barrel of his own gun.

"Seems like you left a few details out of this escape plan you had in mind for me. I ought to drop you where you stand."

"You just do that, Kincaid. Then they'll hang you for murder instead of cattle rustling."

Lance knew the sheriff was right. He couldn't afford to take a chance on anybody believing his side of the story.

"You just hand that gun over and we'll forget this whole affair." Turner evidently doubted that Lance was going to go along with that suggestion.

Even as he spoke, he swung his left arm across his body and smashed it into Lance's right wrist. He moved surprisingly fast for a big man. His speed caught Lance by surprise, and the gun went skidding across the floor. Both men stood staring at each other.

"You are going to hang for cattle rustling, and I'm the witness they need to convict you. I've been tailing you ever since you hit town looking for Kincaid."

"So you're one of the men that have been following me."

"What do you mean one of the men? Christian ain't sent nobody but me. You must be running scared, boy; let's see what you're made of when you don't have a gun in your hand."

Turner stepped in and caught Lance on the side of his head with a crashing right hand. The blow sent Lance against the wall, and his mind went reeling. He tried to shake the flashing lights out of his head as he moved away from Turner. If it hadn't been for the wall, Lance would have been laid out on the floor.

Turner, knowing the blow did a number on Lance, moved in to finish him off. Lance knew he was in no condition to muster up a good punch. As he saw the big man moving toward him, he dropped to the floor and rolled into Turner's knees. Turner's forward momentum sent him flying across the hallway and into the opposite wall. That gave Lance the time he needed to collect his wits and clear his mind. He realized he could not take another solid punch. Turner was too big and too strong. As Turner stepped in to land that finishing blow Lance slipped under it and connected with a hard right hook to the ribs. It sounded like someone walking on crackers as several ribs fractured. Lance followed with a left uppercut that stood the sheriff on his toes. Turner recovered enough to land a glancing right cross to Lance's jaw, but the fight was out of him, and it had little effect. Lance finished the big man with two quick jabs to the nose and a right cross to the chin. After dragging the unconscious Sheriff into a cell and locking it, Lance went to the wash stand, wiped the blood from his face, dusted off his hat and returned to his cell.

CHAPTER 19

Judge Tayler and Payne entered the jail just after sunrise to find the sheriff locked in a cell and Lance resting on a bunk in an unlocked cell with a six-shooter in his belt. Both men's faces showed signs of the scuffle. Lance rose to greet them, explained what had happened, and handed his gun to Judge Tayler.

"I have no reason to doubt your story, and every reason to believe it, considering the circumstances," the judge said. "However, it is your word against his, and it will have to be up to a jury to decide the truth."

Lance told Judge Tayler he was concerned for his safety because of what he discovered on the Rocking R Ranch.

"There's certainly good reason for his concern

since they tried to lynch him last night," Payne said.

"You're not going to take the word of a cattle thief, are you, Judge?" Turner blurted out through his swollen jaw.

"And just what is your version of what happened to put you in this predicament?" asked the judge.

"Ahhh, well, I came in to feed the prisoner. When I opened the cell to give him his food, he overpowered me, took my gun, and wopped me with it. I passed out and just woke up as you came into the jail."

"It will be a frosty Friday before I'll buy that story, Turner. If you were feeding the prisoner, where is the food tray? Your bruises look more like a fair and square beating with fists not a pistol. Finally, how can you explain Mr. Kincaid sitting here all night in an open cell, armed and waiting for the authorities?"

Bull Turner just stood there, dumbfounded, and could think of no reasonable response to the judge's challenges.

Lance appealed again to Tayler. "Judge, whoever is behind this—and I have some ideas about that—can't afford to let me get to trial. If I am allowed to tell my story, and it checks out, it will be the end of their land-grabbing scheme. It will also likely land someone with a murder charge. My partner should be on his way with some federal support, but I'm not sure how soon they will get here."

"It sounds like, if we can delay the trial until the federal authorities get here, we'll be having a trial, but it won't be for you," the judge said. "I brought two deputies up with me from Salado. I think we will just take you back to Salado to wait for your partner and the federal soldiers."

"I would certainly appreciate that, Judge," Lance replied.

"I think I'll round up a few good citizens to come along, just in case anyone gets ideas about waylaying you," Payne said.

The judge nodded in approval. "Good idea. I'll deputize them. Some of those citizens may just decide to take a look at the herd on the Rocking R Ranch while they are nearby. I believe I could issue a search warrant based on the allegations made by Mr. Kincaid.

"Turner, I will be deputizing one of the local citizens to take over your responsibilities until we get this mess cleared up. In the meantime, I think you should stay under lock and key for your own protection."

"Protection from who?" Turner protested.

"You know the answer to that better than we do. If you would decide to share that information with me, it would save 'due process' a lot of time and money."

Turner fell silent.

"Mr. Kincaid, if you're ready, I think we should be on our way," the judge said.

"I'm past ready, Judge. Let's head out. The

sooner we get this settled, the sooner I can see to my father's killer."

"I'm going to allow you to retrieve your guns. You may need them on our way to Salado. But you must agree to turn them over to me when we reach the Salado jail."

"You have my word, Judge."

While the judge woke one of the locals and deputized him, Lance strapped on his six-shooter, grabbed his rifle from the jail rack, and headed to the livery stable to saddle his horse, under the escort of one of Judge Tayler's deputies. Within an hour, the judge, the deputies, Payne, along with three newly deputized locals, and Lance were on the trail to Salado. The horses were fresh and anxious to move out, so they headed south at a brisk trot. The sun had been up for several hours, and the day was warm and sunny. Lance would have reason to be grateful for the bright sunshine soon enough.

About two hours into their trek, they entered an area of the trail that wound between two hills that sloped gently away to a height of several hundred feet. There were patches of hackberry trees and cottonwoods that broke up the fields of grass. The judge and Payne rode in the lead, followed by Lance. The judge's original deputies and the three sworn in at Belton brought up the rear. Because of their number, the deputies may have felt a false confidence. For whatever reason, they were too busy talking to each other to pay proper attention to their surroundings.

Lance, on the other hand, was well aware of the threat he posed to whoever was behind the thieving of his father's land. He also knew that Turner had overheard him tell the judge that federal troops were on their way, and he was sure Turner would get that information to whoever bought and paid for his badge. They could not afford to have Lance and the judge meet up with the troops.

Lance surveyed the hills just ahead, trying to anticipate the next moves of his adversaries. Far to the south, on the bluff of the highest hill, Lance saw a bright reflection. The only thing in nature that could reflect sunlight that way was hunks of mica. Since he had seen no mica in the area, he guessed that he was seeing the work of metal, and that metal likely belonged to a rifle. They were still out of range, but wouldn't be for long.

"Gentlemen!" Lance called sharply. "I think we are riding into trouble. There is a welcoming party waiting for us on the bluff just to the south. I suggest we ride as though we are unaware until we reach that river bank just ahead. Judge, then you give the signal, and we will all hightail it to the protection of that bank."

"I don't see anything, Mr. Kincaid, but I'll take your word for it. I'll call it," the judge said.

They rode on about a hundred yards. As they approached the river bank, the judge yelled out, "Now!"

At the judge's signal, the men wheeled their

horses around and headed for the river bank. The sudden move caught those lying in wait off guard. Shots rang out just as they reached cover.

"Thank God for your keen senses," the judge said to Lance as they dismounted and got into position to return fire.

"I'm afraid we're still in a bad situation. They have the high ground, and we can't make a move without them seeing us," Lance said grimly.

Lance guessed there to be five of them, from the gunfire coming off the ridge. Looking over the situation, he decided that one of them would need to flank the scoundrels and try to get a vantage point to fire from. Otherwise, they were wolf meat. It was just a matter of time.

"Judge, I'm going to make a run for that grove of cottonwood trees. If I can make it there, I'll be able to move through it to their right. From there, I may be able to do some damage. When I light out, try to pin them down."

"You'll get yourself killed," the judge said.

"That's not part of my plan, Judge. I don't kill that easy. 'Sides, if I do, that will just save you a trial."

"You've got sand. I'll give you that, Kincaid."

"Start shooting," Lance yelled as he headed for the grove of trees about one hundred feet away. Several bullets kicked up dirt at his feet as he dashed across the opening and made a final dive for cover. He quickly jumped to his feet and began to make his way through the underbrush and deadfall.

He heard a footstep behind him; before he could react, a crashing blow fell on the back of his head. As
the light dimmed and he felt his legs buckle, his last
thought was, "There must have been six of them."

CHAPTER 20

The route that Colonel Chandler had taken to reach Belton took them very near the grazing land of the Rocking R Ranch. They were just south of Salado when they came upon a small herd of Rocking R cattle.

"Hefty, I think it would be worth our time to stop long enough and check out the running-iron work done on these cattle. If I can verify that, I'll have no trouble supporting Lance's claim to the ranch," the colonel said.

"Good idea, Colonel, but don't take too long. I'm beginning to feel a little uneasy about Lance up there in Belton."

The colonel had one of his men put down a heifer. They began skinning it next to the brand. The evidence was clear. It was obvious that the brand had been altered as Lance had claimed.

"I've seen enough. Let's move out to Belton," the colonel said. As they rode just north of Salado, the colonel rode up alongside Hefty.

"It's been more than twenty years since I've ridden this trail. Luke and I spent a lot of hours in the saddle covering this ground," he said as he looked over the familiar landscape. "Luke had a fierce tug of war going on in his gut. On the one hand, he had sworn to protect the settlers streaming into the territory. On the other hand, he felt a deep concern for the Comanche who were being driven off their hunting grounds. It seemed to Luke to be a needless movement by the settlers motivated by the desire for more wealth and land."

"There is nothing new about that," Hefty replied, as he shook his head. "President Jackson faced the same problem in the East some years back. He discovered he was powerless in preventing the settlers from taking over the Indian lands. He had laws passed to prevent it, but the authorities in the area would not enforce the laws. Even when they did, the juries let the offenders off."

"It seems like times change but people don't. I'm afraid we haven't learned much from our past mistakes," the colonel said in disgust.

"I agree, colonel. Back then, Jackson knew he had only three choices. He could move the Indians to reservations on land the white man was not interested in, he could try to 'civilize' them with education and Christianity, or he could totally eliminate them. I think Mr. Jackson's heart was in the right place. He just didn't know how to handle the problem, so he decided to address the symptoms and to move them west. I wonder if he knew that it was only going to end up being a problem to be handled by those that came after him?"

"Well, guess what, Hefty? We came after him, and we had to handle it and to tell you the truth, we are not doing much better than he did."

"Back in Pittsburgh, my daddy always said, 'the meek shall inherit the earth.' After all those years in the coal mines, I never tried to dash his hopes, but what readin' of history I done, told me in the long run, it was the survival of the fittest. Those with the mostest got the bestest."

"You're right, Hefty, but that doesn't make it right. In time, I hope this nation will take stock of itself and try to right some of its wrongdoings. The freeing of the slaves was a good start, but we haven't begun to think about the hardships we have put upon the Indians. This country was founded on the principles of liberty, freedom, and justice for all. It's time we started living our conscience."

"It will be a tough row to hoe. We haven't learned to be fair and just to our own kind yet. Look what the rascals did to Lance's pa."

"I'm not in a position to solve the nation's problems, but I can damn sure solve this one. Maybe that will be a start of bigger and better things," the colonel said. "Before I finish this, Lance will have his father's ranch back, and Luke's killer will be hung."

"You may get his ranch back, but you'll have to hurry to hang the back shooter before Lance gets to him first."

"One way or the other, that no-account will be brought to justice," the colonel said.

"You got that right, Colonel."

As they rode along in silence, Hefty thought of what the colonel had said about Luke Kincaid. It seemed as though Lance had a lot of his father's teaching in him. Lance sure had a soft spot in him for the Indians. He had shown that when they had the run-in with Two Ponies. Lance was always one to give men the benefit of the doubt, but Katie bar the door, if someone crossed him. He and his pa were sure ones to walk the river with.

They were about two hours from Belton when Hefty pulled up and said, "Did you hear that shootin?"

The colonel called for a halt and listened. After a few seconds he heard a number of shots being fired. "I hear it now. Sounds like it's coming from the far side of that bluff. Let's check it out. Move out at the gallop, men."

As they approached the bluff, they spotted five men positioned behind some large boulders firing on the trail below. When the men saw the uniforms approaching, they turned toward the soldiers. For an instant, they seemed to consider shooting it out with the troops, but thought better of it and lowered their guns as the colonel rode up to them, careful not to expose himself to whatever lay below on the trail.

It didn't take much to see that the men were of less than sterling character and up to no good.

"Having a little target practice, boys?" the colonel asked coolly.

Not a one of the five responded. Hefty moved closer to the edge of the bluff, still keeping himself out of sight. He shouted, "Hello the trail, we are federal troops. Identify yourself."

Below the judge was wondering why the shooting had stopped from the bluff. He was relieved, but remained cautious when he heard the call from the bluff. He identified himself and his men, but stayed out of view.

Colonel Chandler collected the weapons of the ruffians and had one of his men gather up their horses.

"Let's just walk on down and meet these gentlemen you were anxious to kill," he said, and called down to the judge, "Hold your fire. We are bringing down your greeting party for you to identify."

As the colonel and his men approached the judge, Tayler recognized Chandler. He lowered his rifle and stepped out in the open.

"Sure glad to see you, Colonel. It's been a while, but your timing for a revisit couldn't be better. We were on our way to deliver a prisoner to the Salado jail, but it seems these gentlemen had other plans for him."

"Do you recognize any of these men, Judge?" the colonel asked.

"No, I don't. They are not from Salado. Perhaps

they are from Belton. Mr. Payne, do you know any of these men?"

Payne looked them over, then shook his head. "I don't know them by name, but I recognize a couple of them. They drifted into town about a week ago. They seemed to have a lot of business at the courthouse. They bought supplies at my place, along with Slade Cannon, whom they called Daily."

"Why does that not surprise me?" Hefty asked. "Which of these men is your prisoner?"

In all the commotion, the judge had forgotten about Lance. He quickly looked around and realized that Lance had not come back after the shooting stopped. He thought perhaps he was not such a good judge of character after all.

"None of these men are the prisoner," he said ruefully. "I'm afraid I made a bad decision in arming him and allowing him to try to circle around the men on the bluff. It looks like his circle was a little bigger than I had planned for him."

Just then, the remainder of the judge's men moved up near him, leading all the horses.

"I guess my prisoner won't get too far. We still have his horse. Spread out, men, and see if you pick up his tracks."

"That wouldn't happen to be your prisoner's horse, would it?" Hefty asked.

"Yes, it is. Do you know this horse?"

"I know the horse, and I know the owner. Does your prisoner have a name?"

"He is wanted for cattle rustling, and his name is

Lance Kincaid."

By this time Payne had recognized Hefty among the troops. "Judge, this is a friend of Lance. They rode into town several weeks ago. For what it's worth, I'm sure he can vouch for Lance."

Hefty stepped off his horse and walked up to the judge. "I can tell you one thing, Lance is no rustler, and he's no runner either. He is either hurt out there somewhere, or he has been taken against his will to make it look like he is running from the law. Which way did he head to flank these boys?"

The judge pointed to the cottonwood stand. "Last I saw him he was moving into those trees."

"I suggest we start looking there to see if we can find Lance, or enough sign to determine what happened to him," Hefty said.

He moved to the grove of trees, and the judge and his men followed. As they approached the trees, Hefty suggested that only he and the judge move into the grove to prevent the others from covering up what might be clues to the Lance's whereabouts. The judge agreed and followed Hefty. They immediately came upon four freshly rolled cigarette butts.

"Somebody spent time here waiting for somebody or something. I followed one set of tracks in, and there is a second set around these cigarettes," Hefty said in a low voice.

"Check this out," the judge called softly.

Hefty joined him and they stared in silence at bloodstains on the ground.

"There is no sign of a struggle," Hefty said after

a moment. "I'm betting that someone was laying for Lance and hit him from behind. There's blood, but there's no sign of Lance. Wait! It looks like someone was dragged over to these horse tracks."

They examined the tracks, and saw that the ones leading out of the trees made a deeper imprint than the tracks coming in. After about a hundred yards of backtracking, they discovered wagon tracks heading northwest. Hefty noticed the boot prints of two men. Neither were Lance's. The boot size was too small, and the heels were run down, which was one thing that Lance did not abide. Lance had always told Hefty to keep his riding heel in good repair to prevent the boot from slipping through the stirrup if the horse should act up or spook. Nope! These surely were not Lance's boot prints. The ground was disturbed, indicating considerable activity around the wagon tracks. Then Hefty saw the sign he was dreading. About five feet of boot toe marks in the sand indicated that someone had been dragged from the horse to the wagon.

"Judge, it looks to me like someone wanted Lance real bad. They also wanted him alive for some reason. Otherwise, they would have finished him off on the spot," Hefty said.

They decided they had seen all they needed to see, and they returned to the colonel and the other men to discuss a course of action.

"With Lance taken alive, something needs to be done quickly before someone decided he was no longer needed," Hefty said.

"The criminal prosecution is in the hands of the county officers until such time that those officers were proven afoul of the law," the colonel said.

The judge agreed and said, "I feel sure that wrongdoing will surely be found once the colonel has the opportunity to inspect the court records."

Hefty finally interrupted the debate. "This seems like we are talking some kind of political hocus-pocus while my partner's life hangs in the balance. I'm going after the wagon. Anyone who wants to join me is welcome."

"I suggest that Hefty, these deputies, and I follow the wagon tracks, while Colonel, you and your men along with these prisoners proceed to Belton and pay Mr. Christian a visit," the judge said.

The group all agreed, and in minutes they were on their separate ways.

The wagon tracks were easy to follow in the soft dirt. It wasn't long before Hefty decided that he didn't need to see the tracks any farther. The wagon was headed for the Rocking R ranch house.

"My guess is that the wagon has a two-hour head start on us. I'm goin' to head cross country for the Rocking R Ranch. You boys follow the tracks just in case. I'll backtrack and catch up with you if I'm wrong," Hefty said.

CHAPTER 21

Slade was tailing his ambush bunch. When he saw the operation go wrong he headed for town to report it to Christian. Back at the courthouse, Christian was not happy with the report given him by Slade "Daily" Cannon. He was glad to hear that Lance was captured and taken to the ranch house, but he was not pleased that Judge Tayler and the deputies had not been done away with in the canyon. Slade assured him that his men had the group trapped, and it would only be a matter of time until they picked them off one by one.

At the very least, Christian hoped the ambush would give him time to assure that all the other deeds he had forged were safe from question. He was sure he had eliminated everyone who had any legitimate claim to the properties. The Rocking R was the one ranch that could cause him trouble, depending on what Lance knew and who all he had talked to. Christian quickly filled his saddlebags with the cash he had stored in the courthouse safe, the profits from all of his land embezzling. He decided to take it with him when he left for the Rocking R, in case things did not work out as planned with the judge. Then with Lance safe and sound at the ranch house, all he had to do was wait there for Lance's partner to show up looking for him. Christian would put out the word that Lance might be at the Rocking R Ranch, and he figured Hefty would show up soon once he found Lance to be missing. . Hefty would be the last person that might know enough to cause him trouble over the Rocking R. It would be bad enough to lose the ranch, but being tied to the death of Luke Kincaid could really mean the end for him.

The colonel and his men were just entering Belton when they saw a lone rider heading south out of town. The rider was Slade "Daily" Cannon, and he was moving out at a good pace. Christian had sent him on ahead to the ranch. He didn't want Slade to see the cash he was about to stash in his saddlebags.

Chandler and his men crossed the bridge and came to a halt in front of the courthouse. He and his sergeant dismounted and had one of his men take the prisoners to the jail. They dusted themselves off as they ascended the stone stairs of the courthouse. When they entered the public area of the building, they found no one present, but the door to the records room was open. The colonel strode through the large solid oak doors to find Christian filling his saddlebags with cash. The look of surprise on Christian's face was not missed by Colonel Chandler.

"I am Colonel Angus Chandler, and this is Sergeant Wilson. We are here to investigate allegations of fraud concerning the property of a Salado rancher by the name of Luke Kincaid. Whom do I have the pleasure of addressing?"

After a moment of hesitation, Christian replied, "I am Hiram Christian, a Bell County municipal judge. Sure glad to see you, Colonel. I have been warned that there are some ne'er-do-wells in the area up from Three Forks, and I was about to take these funds from the county vault to the bank for safekeeping."

"That won't be necessary," the colonel said briskly. "You can return the money to the vault. I will keep my men here to look after its safekeeping."

"Certainly, Colonel, I am relieved that you are here to see after our safety."

Christian slowly and methodically removed the money from the saddlebags and returned it to the safe. As he did so, his mind was reeling with thoughts of how he was going to handle questions about the Kincaid ranch. He wondered how much the colonel knew, and why he was focused on that particular piece of land. Surely Tayler or Lance couldn't have made it to Austin. Christian swallowed hard, his hand shaking slightly as he relocked the safe. At this point, the profits from his two years of land manipulations were forgotten, and he began to worry about his survival. Thinking fast, he turned to Chandler with a smile.

"It's good timing on your part to be asking about the Rocking R Ranch. There were two men here asking about the deed to that ranch, and it has caused me to do some investigating of my own into the proper ownership," Christian said.

"I'd like to see that deed, if you don't mind," the colonel said.

Christian went to the files and put on a good act of searching for the deed. "Ah! Here it is."

He removed the deed from a brown envelope and handed it to the colonel.

The colonel looked over the document carefully, as he had done with countless others over the past few months. It certainly seemed to be a legal deed, written up in the proper format and on the standard paper stock for such documents. After reading the text of the deed he studied the signature lines.

"Would you mind lighting that oil lamp on the desk?" the colonel asked.

Christian found a match, extended the wick, and lit the lamp. After a few seconds the lamp reached full glow. Chandler took the deed over to the lamp and held the area of the signature line over the chimney.

"Mr. Christian, come over here. You need to see this." Christian approached the lamp and looked down at the deed.

"What am I supposed to be seeing, Colonel?"

"Look closely at the signature line. Many times when a document is signed, particularly if it is signed by a man, the pressure of the pen reduces the thickness of the paper where the signature is made. When light is placed in back of the paper, the signature is distinguishable. What do you see on this signature line?"

To his amazement, Christian could clearly see the signature of Luke Kincaid under the current inked signature of Slade Cannon. "It looks as though Mr. Cannon has some answering to do," Christian said.

"Do you have any idea where we might find Mr. Cannon?"

Christian needed to buy as much time as possible. He had to find a way to get word to Slade that Chandler was onto the fraud, and that troops were on their way to the ranch.

"I have often seen him at the hotel saloon. We could see if he is there now. In the meantime, I will go to the sheriff and have him make out a warrant for Mr. Cannon's arrest. Mr. Caldwell works at the front desk of the hotel. He would recognize Cannon, and could point him out if he is in the saloon. I will see the sheriff and meet you at the saloon."

Chandler studied Christian, wondering if he should trust the concerns Hefty had expressed about the judge. It seemed that Christian was as anxious as anyone to get to the bottom of this fraud. Still, his story about taking the cash to the bank played a little thin. The colonel decided to give him the benefit of the doubt, for the time being, but to keep an eye on the man just the same.

Christian entered the jail and walked quickly over to Sheriff Turner in his cell. The appointed deputy was out of the office. Christian found the keys to the cell, and released Turner. It was obvious that something big had come up. Christian looked pale. His forehead was wet with perspiration, and he was wringing his hands.

"What's up, Christian?"

"We have a problem that needs immediate attention. There's a colonel here from Austin who seems to be onto the Rocking R Ranch deal. Right now, they think that Slade was behind it. I need you to make out a warrant for Slade's arrest. Then I need you to get out to the ranch and warn him. He needs to make himself scarce. Tell him to lay low with the boys at Three Forks, and I will contact him when this blows over."

"Forgery is one thing, but what about Luke Kincaid's shooting? They are sure to tie that to us also."

"That's why Slade needs to get out, and now. Things may work themselves out. When and if they do, we can send word to him. I found out that Lance is Kincaid's son. Things would be a lot cleaner if we didn't have him breathing down our necks. Tell Slade to have one of the boys take care of Lance. We might get lucky and have that sidekick find him by now, and we can get rid of both of them. That would eliminate any legal claims and witnesses concerning the ranch."

"It looks like time for all of us to clear out. Hanging around is just inviting a rope," Turner said.

Christian shook his head. "Running now would be a sure admission of guilt. If we can get Slade out of reach, they will think he is behind the whole affair. With Lance out of the way, we still have a chance to have the county take over the ranch for unpaid taxes. Once it's in the county's hands, we can buy it back for a song. That land is the best in the county, and we could turn a million dollars on it within five years. Now do as I say. Make out the warrant. I will take the troops the long way to the ranch. Ride to the ranch through Live Oak Canyon, and you should beat us to the ranch by an hour or so. That will give Slade enough time to take care of Lance and hit the trail for Three Forks. If Lance's sidekick has not shown up, we will take care of him later."

Turner had his doubts about Christian's plan, but he couldn't think of anything better to do, so he made out the warrant, handed it to Christian, and headed for the livery stable to saddle up and head for the ranch.

CHAPTER 22

Hefty stopped on a bluff overlooking the Rocking R ranch house. Things seemed quiet, almost too quiet. For the last three miles or so he had felt like he was being followed, but he couldn't be certain. Then he saw him. At first glance he thought it was Lance, then he realized it was the man he had seen in Salado when Lance was talking to Judge Tayler. The lone rider was four or five hundred yards away on top of a rolling hill to the south. He had a good view of Hefty and the ranch house. Hefty looked away at the valley below. When he looked back south, the rider was gone.

Although he couldn't ignore the rider, he felt he had to focus on the ranch house, where he was sure they had taken Lance. Hefty moved off the ridge and away from the skyline. He squeezed gently on his pony's ribs, and they headed slowly toward the ranch house, always keeping a grove of trees between him and the house. Just as he was riding into a stand of live oak, he caught a bright reflection coming from the rocks just south of the ranch house. It looks like they are expecting company, he thought grimly. He had looked the area over before he entered the valley, and was sure he could work his way behind the ranch house through a brake of hackberries and into the rocks behind the "welcoming party" without being seen. He had to move quickly, though, because whoever was out there would be expecting to see him ride out on the east side of the oaks.

He tied his horse, removed his spurs, and in seconds he was behind the cabin, moving like an Apache toward the boulders. As he passed the ranch house, he heard voices. He breathed a sigh of relief. It was Lance talking to someone, but he couldn't make out what was being said. At least Lance was alive. He decided he had to take care of the rifleman in the rocks first, and then circle back and check out the ranch house. He continued to make his way to where he thought the reflection originated. As he moved between a large pair of rocks, he saw him. Not thirty feet away was a lone gunman lying in wait.

"Waiting for anyone in particular?" Hefty said.

The gunman swung around, only to look down the barrel of Hefty's revolver.

"Very slow and careful-like, drop your rifle, unbuckle your gun belt, and let it fall. I tend to be the real nervous type. One quick move and you're buzzard bait."

The gunman did as he was told.

"I know you have my partner in that ranch house. I can't think of a good reason not to finish you here and now before I take care of whoever you have in the house with Lance."

The gunman saw Hefty's knuckle begin to turn white as he squeezed the trigger of his six-shooter, and fell apart. "Don't shoot!" he sputtered. "I got no stake in this affair. Cannon is the one you want. He hired us to take care of whoever came after the man we got tied up in there. Then we were to do him in, too."

"Is Cannon in there?"

"No, that's Charlie Jenkins. Charlie and me, we're from Three Forks."

"Three Forks; I thought I knew you from somewhere. Lance and I had a little setto with you and three of your friends on the road to Salado some time back. We should have put you out of your miserable life then. What's your name, or do you have one?"

"Jed, Jed Collins."

"Okay, Mr. Collins, why does Cannon want us dead?"

"We don't know nothin'. We just do what we are bein' paid to do."

"Maybe a 44 slug in the leg would help you with that last answer." Hefty took aim at the man's left leg.

"Okay! Okay! I heard Cannon say that with the two of you out of the way, there would be no one to claim this ranch."

"You heard him say it to who? Is he alone in this?"

Collins clammed up and didn't say a word.

"I guess you don't really need a left leg; you have a right one just like it."

Hefty again took aim at the gunman's left leg. Collins could feel the sweat running down his back under his shirt. All the color had left his face, and his hands were trembling.

"If I say any more, he'll have me killed."

"That's later. I'm going to kill you right now if you don't start talking. Who is the 'he' that's going to have you killed?"

Collins ran his tongue over his dry lips, but it did no good. His mouth felt like it was full of sand. He couldn't take his eyes off of the revolver pointed at him.

"You call it, Pard, talk or die. I can always get the answers from your friend Charlie." He began to increase the pressure on the trigger.

"Christian! It's Christian. Cannon works for Christian."

"Surprise, surprise!" Hefty replied. "All right, Charlie's friend, let's pay a visit to the ranch house."

As Collins turned toward the house, he reached inside his vest for his hideaway gun. Hefty was expecting as much. He took two quick steps toward

Collins and smashed his 44 against Collins's left temple. His legs buckled and he went down in a heap. Hefty took the latigos from Collins's tie-downs and wrapped him up like a Christmas turkey, hands tied behind him and feet tied to his hands. He added a gag by using Collins's neckerchief. He was glad he got the job done without firing a shoot. Chances are the man with Lance was not alerted to any trouble.

Leaving Collins to sleep it off, Hefty took his time to reach the house. . He went from tree to boulder to tree, slinking like a mountain cat, careful not to step on any dry limbs or leaves. As he approached the back door, he could hear voices inside.

"No use asking me questions. I'm just hired help for Slade Cannon. 'Sides, it won't do you a lick of good. You're a dead man once your partner shows himself."

"What makes you think he's coming?"

"Oh, he's coming. It's just a matter of sooner or later."

Hefty had heard enough. Kicking the back door off its rusty, worn-out hinges, he shouted, "How about sooner?"

Jenkins whirled around, drawing his gun as he turned. He was too late. A 44 slug shattered the middle button on his shirt, and sent him flying back against the wall. He was dead before he hit the plank floor.

"Are you okay, Lance?"

"Outside of a head that feels like it was stomped

on by a longhorn, I'm fine," he said ruefully, but he couldn't hide his relief at seeing Hefty. "Too bad you had to finish off my friend here. I was hoping to get some answers from him."

"Don't worry. Your information is safe and sound, tied up out there in the rocks. This one and Jed out there are two of the hombres we met on our way to Salado. They work for a guy named Cannon."

Hefty told Lance all that had gone on since they had split up. Lance had figured that Christian was behind the land grab, but he still couldn't be sure who had shot his father.

"Lance, the troops are going into Belton to question Christian, and Judge Tayler and his deputies are on their way here. I'll bring our friend in from where I left him for your safekeeping, and then I'll ride out and lead the judge back here to arrest Collins. We can all go back to Belton and take care of Christian and Cannon. Are you up to watching over our neighbor from Three Forks?"

"I'll do a darn site better here than I would ridin' out with this busted head."

Hefty went out to Collins and threw some water in his face. He untied his feet, pulled him up, and marched him back to the house. He had Collins lie down again, and retied his feet, leaving the gag on him, then tied him to one of the posts that supported the ceiling beams.

"Do you recognize this guy?" Lance asked.

"Sure do. He is one of the welcoming party that

greeted us at Three Forks."

"You got that right. His next greeting will be from Judge Tayler."

"He should be safe and sound until we get back. He can sit and look at his dead friend and be thinking how close that was to being him."

Hefty headed back to his horse, mounted up, and headed on the double to meet the judge and his deputies.

Lance's head was throbbing and his body ached. He went to the wash basin and rinsed some of the blood from his head and neck, then soaked a rag and placed it gingerly over the lump on his head that was as big as a hickory nut. Just before he turned away, he caught his reflection in the mirror over the basin. He had sure seen better days. He sat down in a chair with a groan, intending to rest his eyes. In seconds he was fast asleep.

As happened so often with him, he woke with a start while dreaming of that Civil War battle where all of the enemy soldiers looked like him. It still made no sense, and he wondered how long he would be haunted by these images. He looked out the window, wondering how long he had slept; the sun was low on the horizon, so he guessed it had been an hour or more. He was seated across the room from Collins, and was considering removing the gag to get more information when he heard a horse calling from the corral. It could mean another horse was approaching. He guessed it was Hefty and the judge, but just in case, he was glad Hefty had retrieved his gun from the wagon. He checked the loads in his pistol and lifted the six-shooter out of the holster several times to make sure it was free.

The pain in his head had eased and he was feeling much better as he looked out of the front window to see a lone rider in the distance. The rider was making no attempt to conceal himself. He must have been expecting a friendly reception. As the rider drew closer, Lance recognized him. It was Slade "Daily" Cannon. Lance knew from his conversation with Hefty that Cannon was the one who ordered them killed, but he still didn't know how he fit in with his father's death. He didn't seem like the back-shooting type. "Daily" had too much of a reputation as a skilled gunfighter. As Slade stepped off his horse, Lance opened the door and moved out on the porch. He could not help but be amused at the surprised look on Slade's face.

Cannon recovered quickly, and could see from the knot on his head and the blood on his shirt that Lance was in a world of hurt.

"Looks like you're working a bale short of a load," he said to Lance.

Lance ignored his comment and said, "If you're here to see your boys, you're a little late. One is dead and the other is not available right now. He's a mite tied up, so he won't be much help to you."

"I don't need no help. If there's a job to do, I can do it myself." As he spoke he began to move to his right.

"Maybe so, but if you take one more step to get

the sun to your back, it will be your last step."

"It seems to me that's wishful thinking coming from a man with a busted head wearing his blood on his shirt instead of in his insides."

"You're a fool, Cannon. I could beat you on my worst day. Too bad you had to ride such a long way just to die." Lance wasn't sure he believed his own words, but he had to put up a good front to get momentum on his side.

As the two men exchanged challenges, they did not notice the lone rider moving down the hill behind the house. It was the other man who had been shadowing Lance and Hefty ever since they came to this part of the country. He gracefully and quietly slid down from his horse, shucked his rifle from its scabbard, and moved to a position in the trees where he could see both men without being detected by them.

"I should have taken care of you the first time we met, when you were trespassing out here," Cannon said with contempt. "The law will thank me for saving them the trouble of hanging a cattle rustler."

"They might be a sight more pleased to see the territory rid of a bushwhacker who goes around shooting innocent men in the back."

"Your pa was a stubborn old man. He just wouldn't listen to reason. He should have accepted the offer I made him for the ranch."

"So you shot him in the back."

"Them's your words, not mine. If it would have been up to me, he would have gotten it the same way you're going to get it—face to face."

Sheriff Turner saw the two men squared off at each other as he topped the ridge to the north. He was approaching from Lance's back. He had no idea how much time he had to lend a hand to Slade. When he was about two hundred yards away, he dismounted and moved on foot to about one hundred yards away. This is as good a place for a shot as I'm likely to get, he thought. He had already cocked his Winchester when he left his horse, so Lance would not hear the telltale click. Placing the rifle in the fork of a live oak, he took careful aim at Lance's back.

Just as he began to squeeze the trigger, the men ran out of words, and Cannon went for his gun. Lance's draw was so quick, it caused Turner to hesitate for just an instant, and in that instant he felt a stabbing pain in his left side at his middle ribs He flinched as he fired, and hit Lance in the right shoulder. Turner reeled to his left. His lungs were on fire, and he tasted blood as he tried to swallow. He knees buckled, and he was losing consciousness as blood began to replace the air in his lungs. The last sight he saw before he died was the man who had shot him running from the trees toward Lance; his last thought, an unfinished question, "How . . . ?"

Lance's shot was lightning fast and on the mark. Cannon took the slug square in his chest. His own shot was late, and it kicked up a puff of dust as it went harmlessly into the ground. When Lance felt the gun buck in his hand, he knew he had bested Cannon, but he knew he had been shot just as he fired, and he was in a world of hurt. His shoulder felt like someone had fired it with a red-hot branding iron. Bright lights began to flash in his head, and then the daylight began to fade. As he was losing consciousness, his nightmare returned. He could see the image of himself running toward him. Is this the way it will end? When the image reaches me, will I die? Is this the meaning of my nightmares? What will become of Amy? Hefty is a little late getting here. Dark Moon said he would be here. All these thoughts ran through his head as he sank to the ground. The last thing he remembered was someone catching him as he was on his way down. Then there was total darkness and silence.

CHAPTER 23

W e checked the hotel; Cannon was not there," Chandler said as he approached Christian in front of the court house.

"I have the warrant for his arrest," Christian replied. "Since he is not in town, I'm sure he must be at the ranch."

"Then that's where we're heading," the colonel said. "Lead the way. Is the sheriff coming?"

"No. He needs to appear in court at Salado in the morning. We won't be needing him. We have the papers to make the arrest."

"That's it, then. Let's head out."

Christian hesitated for a moment. He had to try to give the sheriff as much of a head start as he could.

"Is there a problem, Mr. Christian?"

"Oh, no. It's just that it is getting late in the day. Perhaps we should hold off and get a good start at daylight."

A local man standing nearby, Mickie Thompson, overheard the judge's comment and said, "Judge, if you take the shortcut through Cedar Canyon, you could beat sunset easy."

"You're right, Thompson," Christian said, trying to hide his annoyance. "That trail was closed because of high water for so long, I forgot about it. Very well, gentlemen, let's be on our way."

Christian's loss of memory about the shortcut and his obvious discomfort at Thompson's reminder put the colonel on guard. He turned to Thompson and said, "Perhaps you could join us?"

Before Thompson could answer, Christian said, "That won't be necessary; I know the way."

"I'm sure you do, but it wouldn't hurt to have an extra hand."

"Whatever you say, Colonel," Christian shrugged.

"I'd be happy to join you, Colonel. I never did trust that Slade Cannon. I'd be glad to be around to see him get what's coming to him," Thompson said.

The group headed off at the trot with Thompson in the lead. The colonel eyed Christian; it didn't appear that Christian was anxious to get to the ranch. He seemed to be a little on edge after that last conversation. After hearing about the back shooters, the colonel decided he was happy to see Christian ahead of him as they moved out to the ranch.

CHAPTER 24

Hefty was returning to the ranch with the judge and his deputies when they heard the gunfire. "That sounded like it came from the ranch house," Hefty said. "Something has gone wrong."

"Lead the way," the judge called out.

Hefty urged his horse into a dead run, and the others followed in close pursuit.

It was all over by the time they arrived. They came upon the sheriff first. He was lying dead in the bloodstained sand, a small hole in his left side, his right side blown wide open. As they covered the last hundred yards, they found Cannon lying face down in the dirt with his gun still in his hand.

Just in front of the porch was a man dressed in the gray trousers of the Confederate Army, on his knees holding Lance in his arms. He turned to face

Hefty, and Hefty stopped in his tracks.

"Lance is in a bad way, we need to get him to a doc fast," the man said to Hefty.

Hefty stared at him, dumbfounded.

When Hefty did not move, the man urged impatiently, "I'll explain later. Right now we need to get those horses hitched to the wagon."

Hefty gathered up his wits, caught up the horses, hitched them to the wagon, spread some blankets out in the wagon, and helped the stranger lift Lance into it.

As the colonel and his group approached the ranch house, they saw Hefty and a stranger placing a man in a wagon that was hitched up and ready to roll. Christian recognized Cannon's body lying in the dust, and knew that something had gone wrong. He slowly began to fall back as the group picked up their pace. The attention of the group was focused on the activity ahead, and his movement was not noticed.

"What's going on here, Hefty?" the colonel asked as he rode up and stepped off his mount.

"Lance is bad shot; we need to get him to the doc. The judge can explain what happened here. We need to get help for Lance. We'll head for Doc Barton in Salado. Did you see Christian in Belton?"

"Sure, we did. He's right—he was with us just a minute ago. What happened to him?"

"I'm not surprised he took off out of here when he saw his hired gun in the dirt," Hefty said. "One of Cannon's men spilled the beans about this whole thing to save his own hide. But first things first. We need to get Lance taken care of." Hefty and the stranger took off for Salado with their horses tied behind. As they departed, Hefty called back, "You'll find a man tied up in the ranch house. Keep him locked up until we meet up."

"Colonel," the judge said, "We best get back to Belton and straighten out this ranch deed, and try to catch up with Christian.

"I agree. Sergeant, assign two men to bring these three bodies into Belton. We'll take the prisoner with us."

"Yes sir."

Judge Tayler explained to the colonel what had gone down before he got there. He repeated what Hefty had told him about Jenkins and Collins holding Lance and waiting to waylay Hefty. He also told him how, apparently, the lone rider that left with Hefty had intervened by killing the sheriff just as he fired at Lance from behind.

Collins, the prisoner, later told the judge that he and Jenkins were hired by Cannon, and that Cannon and the sheriff were on Christian's payroll. He said that Cannon called out Luke Kincaid and Kincaid refused to sell his ranch at the price offered. Before it could come to a fair and square shoot-out between Cannon and Kincaid, Christian shot Luke from behind. He explained that Christian had Cannon's name put on the deed to remove any suspicion from him. It looked to the judge like Lance saved the county the trouble of hanging Cannon. Collins also confessed Cannon was the leader of that nasty bunch holed up at Three Forks.

The following day the judge went to see Hefty at Dr. Barton's and told him that Lance would have a reward coming for killing Cannon.

"He can always use the money, but that's not going to satisfy him. You can bet he'll be lookin'to get Christian," Hefty said.

"He's going to have to get well before he does any lookin'," the judge said.

Hefty smiled and said, "He'll recover, you can count on that. He's tougher than an old bull buffalo hide."

CHAPTER 25

Three days had passed since they got Lance to Doc Barton. He had lost a lot of blood, and he was barely hanging on for the first two days. Just as things were looking up for Lance, he came down with a fever that nearly finished him. On the third day he was in and out of consciousness, and was able to take on a little broth. Hefty stayed by his side day and night for the three days.

The afternoon of the fourth day, Hefty decided that Lance was well enough to be brought up to date on the happenings of the past week. As Hefty entered the room with the man who had saved Lance's life, Lance woke from a restless sleep. It was Lance's nightmare all over again. He saw himself standing before him, but something was different this time. As he looked to the other man in the room, he also saw Hefty.

"Lance, say hello to Len, your twin brother."

Lance just lay there, staring at Len Kincaid. After a full minute he took two deep breaths, and his face showed total amazement. For a few seconds his mind went reeling through the past. He saw his life reviewed before him, and for a moment was unaware of anything around him. Finally he looked at Hefty, then at Len.

"I remember! Now I remember! After all these months of trying to remember—and now it is as though I never forgot. Pa was a Texas Ranger, and Ma died of the fever when we were eight years old."

"Yeah," Len replied. "Pa, you, and I bought the ranch and moved from Austin when Pa left the Rangers."

Lance smiled and said, "You were always more of a rancher than I was, so I decided to follow Pa's footsteps and join the Rangers."

"You'd probably still be a Ranger if it hadn't been for the war."

"My mind is flooded with all the pictures of my past. It seems as though it all happened in a day, instead of thirty years. I even remember you, Hefty."

"Well, it's nice to know I fit in there somewhere."

Hefty and Len looked at each other and smiled.

"At last, my nightmare makes sense," Lance said. Then he added cautiously, watching his brother, "I remember that we had some pretty harsh words over the war, and about who was in the right and who was in the wrong. We didn't part on good terms when we each left to join up. I realized that your issue was states rights, but mine was slavery. I was tormented over our difference during the war. Then came the battle of Five Forks in Virginia. You didn't see me, but I saw you, just before I was blown to hell by your artillery. Your face was the last image I saw before I passed out. I've been seeing it over and over again in my nightmares, all these months." He took a deep breath, then asked, "Why didn't you come to me when Hefty and I arrived in Belton?"

Len hesitated, pushed his hat back on his head, and said, "I wanted to, Lance, but our differences were so intense when we parted, I wasn't sure how much you had been siding with the Reconstruction of the South. I made my way back home about six months after the war, and headed straight for the ranch. I found Pa's body just off the road into the ranch." Len swallowed hard. "It had been there a spell. The only way I recognized him was from his watch that you and I bought him. I bundled up what was left of him, and took him to his favorite tree and buried him. I could see from his vest that he was back shot.

"Since the county was taken over by Yankees, I knew I would not get the time of day from the authorities. It took me a couple of months to find out who was living on our ranch. I stayed shy of Belton and Salado, and just got information from transients who had heard the latest at the local saloons. Once I found out it was Slade Cannon at the ranch, and he was El Jefe of the Three Forks Gang, I wasn't sure what I could do about him without help. Then you came along."

"I was camped north of town when you passed so close to me that I recognized you. I decided to let you play out your hand enough to determine where you stood with that Reconstruction outfit."

"So you were the one shadowing us along with one of Christian's men," Lance said.

"Sure was. I did a better job than Turner. I knew you'd recognize me, but I kept just enough distance between us to keep you guessing about me. I was sure glad when you found Pa's grave."

"Once I saw what was coming down with the sheriff and Christian, I decided that I would be worth more watching your back than I would be joining you. I was about to make a run on the ranch house when I saw Hefty injun up on Collins. I had a hunch that Slade would be coming by before long, but the sheriff was a surprise. I was never much for speed or accuracy with a handgun, but I was always right respectable with the long gun. Unfortunately, I was a shade late getting the sheriff. He is the one who got you from behind."

"What about Cannon?" Lance asked.

"He was on his way to his maker before he hit the ground," Len replied.

"Which one of them shot Pa?" Lance asked.

"That's the bad news," Hefty replied. "Collins

did some talking to save his neck. He claims it was Christian who bushwhacked your pa. Colonel Chandler thought that Christian was with his bunch, but when they went looking to ask him about the shooting, they realized he was nowhere to be found. By the time the colonel got back to Belton, Christian was gone, and so was all the cash from the courthouse safe."

"Do they know which way he headed, Hefty?" Lance asked.

"Not for sure, but Christian was doing a lot of talking about the silver that was being mined out in the New Mexico Territory. I think it was a town called Pinos Altos. "You can be sure if that's where he is headed, it will be to cheat the people out of their ore, and not to mine it himself."

"I guess I'll be paying a visit to Pinos Altos," Lance said, as he tried unsuccessfully to get out of bed.

"You won't be paying a visit anywhere for a spell, Mr. Kincaid," Doc Barton said as he entered the room.

"It looks like my business with Christian will have to wait," Lance said ruefully, leaning back against the pillows. "In the meantime, Len, let's get the ranch ownership cleared up."

"The legal papers are already in the works, thanks to Colonel Chandler, who was an old friend of Pa's."

"Len, someone will need to stay here and get the ranch back on its feet. Would you volunteer for that job?"

"Won't you need me with you if you go after

Christian? I'm sure he will have some hired guns by the time you catch up with him."

"We can handle Christian and his crew," Hefty replied.

"Who's 'we'? You don't have a stake in this fracas. There's no sense in you risking your neck," Lance said.

"You got to be putting the shuck on me, Lance. After all we been through, do you think I can walk away without writing the last chapter to this affair?"

"I have to admit, I wouldn't be here today if you hadn't been around to save my hide. It grieves me some, because I don't like to be beholden to any man. I guess I'm getting a good lesson on the value of friends. I surely do accept your offer. I'd be downright pleased to have you with me."

"You'd have a hard time getting rid of me."

"That settles it, then. Len, you look after our holdings, and Hefty, you get our supplies ready and ask around about this Pinos Altos, and the best way to get there."

Later, Hefty had met with Colonel Chandler, who was still in Bell County finishing up the necessary formalities covering his action involving the Kincaid Ranch. Hefty told the colonel about Lance's intentions of going after Christian as soon as he was well enough.

A few days later, the colonel came by to visit Lance

"I'm Colonel Chandler. How you feeling, Lance?" he asked as he entered Lance's room.

BELL COUNTY BUSHWHACKERS

"I'm glad to meet you, sir. Hefty told me all you have done for me and my father's ranch. I thank you for that. I feel like I've been rode hard and put up wet, but I'm feeling a little better each day. I expect I'll be up and at 'em soon."

Chandler took a seat by Lance. "There is no need to thank me. It was not only my duty, I had a personal interest in it because your father and I were good friends. We rode together as Texas Rangers. He was a good man. One of the best."

"The man who shot him from ambush is going to answer to me," Lance replied.

"That's what I wanted to talk to you about. I understand you intend to pursue Christian into the New Mexico Territory."

"You got that right. He is going to pay for killing Pa."

"Lance, you realize as a common citizen in New Mexico, you will have no grounds to take legal action against Chandler."

"Then I'll take illegal action against him."

The colonel shook his head. "There is a better way. If you will take the oath to abide by the law and make every effort to bring Chandler to a fair trial, I will swear you in as a U.S. Marshal. I have the approval of President Johnson to do so".

"I would appreciate that, Colonel. I have no problem with the oath, just as I didn't as a Ranger."

With that agreement, the colonel administered the oath to Lance, and provided him with a badge and the papers to identify him as a U.S. Marshal. He also included a warrant for Christian's arrest.

Colonel Chandler made the same offer to Hefty, but he declined. He told the colonel that he was just buying a ticket for the show, but he didn't intend to be one of the players. Two weeks later, Lance and Hefty were off to the New Mexico Territory. Hefty had worked out the best route to get there, but Lance had added a small side trip that would take them through Fort Griffin.

"I can't figure why you'd want to take the long route to New Mexico by going to Fort Griffin," Hefty said with a smirk on his face as he watched Lances face for a reaction.

"The reason you're going is to gather as much information about the New Mexico Territory as you can. From what I hear, the more we know the better chance we have to keep our scalps. You darn sure know the reason I'm going."

"I guess it's to give you more days to hear the stories I haven't told you yet."

"On second thought maybe a shorter route would be better," Lance said as he slapped Hefty on the back and urged Bess into a lope.